Eternity

ETERNITY

John Fraser

AESOP Modern Fiction
Oxford

AESOP Modern Fiction
An imprint of AESOP Publications
Martin Noble Editorial / AESOP
28a Abberbury Road, Oxford OX4 4ES, UK
www.aesopbooks.com

First paperback edition published by AESOP Publications
Copyright (c) 2025 John Fraser

www.johnfraserfiction.com

A catalogue record of this book is
available from the British Library.

First hardback edition 2024

ISBN: 978-1-914938-36-8

Contents

AFTER LIFE

We love the birds. They ornament our lives, they make us grow in tune with them, with almost everything: music, flight. They – are indifferent. If they could, they would resent how we have hunted and harassed them, killed their food, and poisoned them. By good luck – they don't seem able to do that sum.

Maybe – there's sums we can't do either.

Or – they could be the aliens we seek, flown here from different stars. The journey back?

'No! Not yet.' Why? When, then?

Which tiny opening of silver light to aim at, which one did you come from ... does it matter? Yes, of course.

So – we aren't alone, and nor are they ... what's next?

I despised pop concerts.

The first one I went to, the lights and the beat were wonderful, you couldn't have imagined them, not anywhere. It was a universe, the one you'd not believed in since you were promised it when you were a child. The eager people, not your friends but not overtly hostile – they were everywhere, and if you went alone, whatever you started as, you climbed on the eagle's back, all of you – each with their eagle, and their loneliness, and beside me there was another me: 'I love you,' I said. 'What?' she said. I held her hand, like the music said, and at first this other me, her pinched Polish face like a bit of space-rock, gypsum, lit up by the days as the nights swept past and blackened it with soot – it took me in as part of the collectivity. But we went out together at the end, and I did love her, and being straight was the best thing, better than nothing like had been before the dull pulse-plodding music and the lights and the whipping us on by the singer and the backing group that really could sing and didn't mind being under his, the lead hero's, spreading tree all evening, and mine was real true love, and it was the worst thing that ever happened to me, and I fell into the spider's trap, and couldn't get out of her terrible story that dribbled over me, sticky, leaking from a Polish coffin underground....

Anna. She was your box, and the soil on top. You were trapped beneath her, beside her.

'Anna?' asks Buryat, shaping up for harsh words: 'She's ordinary, ugly. Once "plain", now, honestly – a fright. Emaciated, muscular – if you had a three-round bout with her, you'd be crying "uncle" after one.'

Her work, lifting, deploying heavy stuff – gives her the strength to pull your head off, to have her wrapped round you like a carpet, and the donkeys will come and trample you, both.

Can being born in Poland be responsible? For anything? Not for Anna, surely....

'All true,' I say: 'She is a lump. Lumps – the sugar of the world, no doubt. Dull, resentful, loud in defence. Too much of her – your organs shudder. But ... the worse there is, the more there is to love. To sacrifice yourself, perhaps, but – human, absolutely human, Buryat!'

I could, on my own, live, I think. But – I don't. The human conditional: ... 'I might – I don't'. What else is there to be prized and valued? *If* I do what I want – would it cost me more than I have? The human state, shaky and ephemeral ... What other animals, so careless of their fellows, make you love them so, forgive them what they didn't do to you but for what they *are*, for ever, for their awful lives that you fell, jumped, into ... They are the twisted stem, and you must free its spirit ... find the tree within.

A slender, elegant, well-bound folio, until you opened her and read.

'You'll regret,' says Buryat, my friend, the spy: 'You think you're strong, like Prometheus. But – you have the choice. Any fool can pick the bad horse, ride it, break it, destroy it, shame yourself. Be different. Bet on the fast, good-looking mare, spend your winnings on Lambrusco and papayas.... Leave Anna to the rodeo....'

Does it reassure you, to know the universe has rules? Does it reassure you, to know there's a criminal code, that binds you too? That the cops can take you off? And you have rules built in – many, many – not like the red and yellow bird, who knows about the family, distances and predators – things that might be useful for you too. You have complicated ones of loyalty, of who you tell what. And Time. What you can't do today you could do yesterday ...

We should discuss them more, these rules – not in a parley of us instruments, in the evening, with alcohol or pot, all melody – but conscious of the overhanging cliff. Fixed there till there's rain or drought, or something that shakes the ground, and down it comes.

Before it decides the punishments, the law says if you're guilty it doesn't matter what you did. You're guilty. Feel it.

Rubbing out a species – it isn't easy, though it's been done countless times. The Creator, the Supreme Showman and Impresario – does a good job with the eraser. Sends the tempests, the landslides, the diseases – into the spiky nests and dusty tunnels. Still, some resist, cling on. The humans – themselves great exterminators – they can't fight back, but don't go easy. They're on the list now, the top. Who's next?

On with the search for perfection. Behold the art show in the universe ... bands of colour, swirls of dust, noxious atmospheres ... humankind is still out there, in front, ingenious and sparky. Multicoloured. It will take time to rid existence of them, of us, and who is next? Wolves, peacocks? – almost everybody has a claim, but most are opportunist, they don't know how to make it plain – how good the world is, how you'd like to gobble down that goodness so you're full of it. The bad – excreted on the ground: with a foot you can cover it with fallen leaves ... Ants, fruit-flies? Do they persist? Worth a modest bet ... Knowing good and bad – that seemed the answer, or the clue ... but no. All that was an invention. More reflection? More self-doubt? Waiting for tomorrow's supreme species – passing the buck, the plugged nickel ...

Ingratiation, that's the best, the only bet.

*

Anna told me how her eyes had a disease ... she had to wear dark glasses or she'd go blind – and not just eyes ... there was a disease profound, and the treatment wore the whole system down. Be very careful – your companion, your sickness, is touchy, kills or blinds you if you don't follow his rules. What he intends, and how he deals with what you have in mind – it's a war you carelessly didn't want; dared to happen. Quite unprepared – ask somebody for help, in debit to them for decades. Too much light? Or fear of it – what it might do, what it might show. A just precaution, anyway, be on guard, respect illumination.

'What's that paper you're studying?' asks Buryat.

'It's an injunction,' I tell him: 'I'm barred from the casino for cheating: from the rest as well – the dogs and horses. I wish I knew how I could cheat at chance....'

'It's your name,' he says: 'The police. They think you are a launderer, wash dirt off what you have, the cash ... believe you pretend you lost it all on the red, the black – the wheel of fortune. Soldiers and shamans – they front almost all the crime ... that should make you lighten up: you'd be no match for them.'

Buryat humours my pretensions. He knows nothing. He says, 'Power and knowledge? – bet against those two, you're a trusting guy: play the shell game with them.'

'It's the great cake-bake, Buryat,' I say: 'Everyone makes one to their recipe, they look like all the others. You don't win, don't know why some guy has. You take the cake home – it's limp and stale. That's why you didn't win? It's inedible. So are all the others – the winner too, that's been consumed, it's been on TV, crumbling putty ... You lost, accept it, it's a lesson ...The ingredients – they are you, they always are.'

It was life: self-pity. No one else is interested.

We were a huge family, underneath the other, even huger, one. Like in an archaic marriage, we were the female part, we had to smile, submit, recover. Minister, comfort, heal.

It had begun an age ago ... my father? A debt, a favour – money and permission to take one of their women, and to take a debt which would for ever grow, and never die, like the sacred flame in Iran, with sacrifices to Ahura Mazda. Don't wait up for Him! He's a platoon! Twenty names, and all creation.

We were bound to believe. If there is a God, or Gods – you have to love them, hate them, no difference. They exist so they can be served. We believed, we had to, in the other, the unholy, family.

So – this other family, an immense, an ever-growing band – we were their tributaries. We hid them, gave them alibis, burned their bloody clothes, fenced their thefts, healed their wounded, buried their victims, gave them shelter, protected them. Love and fear. No love and much fear. Some we liked and all we feared.

When they were on the run, we were the ones who paid, who went to jail, who died for them. We were a tribe, who lived from the dwindling forest stocks, while robbers came and took the trees, the animals. The gangs fought wars, and we were chivvied, they were our totems who we had to protect, with all our being. Die for them.

We had once been fugitives, I suspect. Now we have been hunted down and enslaved, been subjugated, by the gangs. They saw us run, and snaffled us, as slaves, or hostages. It could happen without crime and blackmail: – in the Congo, a certain tribe is despised by, subordinated to, another. To an outsider – they seem similar, symbiotic even. The Aka. They are small, that's all.

With us, it happened in a modern city. No forest, and no trees. We were animals you can milk or skin, but seldom butcher. Our advantage was to be alive, always available and servile. Killing us – a stupidity.

To stop being accomplices, we could back off, back out – go to the forest, where there were few trees, just tubers in the grit: rubbery amphoras. A source of moisture in the long dry season.

We could stop being poor and accomplices, become just – very poor.

Subsist. Attract more people attracted by nothing, living in and on, nothing. Living without: – you make a little troupe, invent the myths, sing the songs. Live on discards, live by the blowpipe – eat little birds, tiny scurrying creatures smaller than outcast rats.

Walk. Cut down the few trees, don't cut baobabs if you can avoid. Devise harsh rules for marriage, for choosing leaders. Work for others by the day, sometimes, to get cash for what you need, can't find or scrounge.

There! No gang would want you now, you're beyond helping anyone, you can't be blackmailed. You are free.

This solution exists in Madagascar. I'd read about it – be so outcast you're protected, preserved, a curiosity. The Mikéa.

You shelter those who run away from civilisation. A thief, a murderer, has more self-respect, enjoys her meals and walking on a pavement. We'd be of no interest to scholars, to anthropology, because it was so very simple. Easy. But we didn't do it.

We were accomplices of the strong, for ever.

*

'Anna was fun,' says Buryat, 'Once. She sang and danced, in Poland. You must have done something to her, broken her. She needed looking after – not luxury, but smooth days. You couldn't ... You give up. You blame others.'

'She was too fragile to be taken over,' I say: 'Already, she subsisted – cutting her rations down would be a cruelty. The sick, those who need care and sometimes even love – too bad! This is not the place, the world, for them.

'She was a precious ceramic in a sack – you couldn't see how she'd been fragmented. Men, women – each uninvited, took their kick.'

*

'Take care,' says the boss, 'Of my friend, the impulsive, careless one. Give him a home, until he wants to leave.'

And that we do. We must.

'No,' Anna says: 'This guy's rubbish. Put him down, and tell the lie. Chop up the corpse. Do everyone a favour.'

*

My cousin took me to Berlin when I was fourteen. We were in a gang, and I went round the clubs, I had a little camera, so small it lodged in my palm, a mouse ... I took photos of the tattoos for one of our associates, for his pattern book. It led me to a lot of sex and one evening, or morning – the guy who ran the girl I was with came in, and found me having free lunch off her, and threw me down into the alleyway, and stopped my heart. We were a company, a community – they rallied round, the guys, mine, his even – and started me off again, like I was a watch, at battery's end. For days I couldn't sit or lie, listen to music, go to bed I was so stiff for how they hit me to start my crown wheel up again. That became the root of my philosophy.

I was smart, and most of the rest were stupid – in Neu-Koln, no one graduated from the elementary school. They were nurses, porters in the hospital, and robbed the corpses and the people going into surgery – then they grew up and there was nothing for them, no work that couldn't be done by twelve-year olds.

You could work in music – easy. Rap and hip-hop it was then, the words, the moves – learnt off by rote. There was money in it, but you could end up shot in a ditch: the competition ... When the money came, the name was 'public money'. The city was like every other big city, so the money poured in to match the bigness: like a dwarf ordered a big suit, stayed small, tiny even, and all who wanted wore the suit which was big, bigger still than all of us, and so the pants, the sleeves, were full of little guys like me, and we would strut down the street, scores of us, animating the one huge suit, all of us the same, all clumsy thieves and bandits.

Rich private guys took over, expelled the tenants and made palaces that didn't work and cost a fortune to bivouac in them.

So, when the time came that I'd decided I must go in the forest, and be no longer in a family, a gang, subordinate, exploited by the bigger, more daring, more thoughtless and more ingenious bosses – you wouldn't say I was an innocent. If I had been, I'd not have considered living off the trees.

'You're bright,' says Buryat: 'Born wrong, paired up bad with Anna; a criminal. But don't fret. You can express yourself, get a dull job, hide from everyone you know ... be a success, sleep in the same bed every night. Find the path out of the labyrinth. How to become yourself, or someone else, completely different.'

It's an idea. Simple or complex? Simple things arouse, but haven't ever worked – justice, truth, equality. They're the best crockery, never ever used.

So – complexity. The city? The intricate, the anthill – but we weren't ants, we never managed coping with the dirtiness, the dust, the shit.

And then – our bosses came, gave me a kicking. On the movies, after boots in the head – you get up, climb the wall. It isn't so. It really hurts, and you can't breathe. So – movies is a false trail. Science? Science has a history, but history – it doesn't have a science.

Science of language, of what we say and how? Words – they're between you and your horse, language comes from people trekking, those carts with solid wheels across the grasslands, hitting the mountains and you settle down and talk. That's it. No philosophy, and only epics – even with a million lines, they all turn out the same, and the magic in them never works a second time ...

If I can't find a place to start – for me, it means there isn't one. There is no remedy. You must re-invent the wheel, over and over – that explains the shape, but not where you it can take you.

'Buryat,' I say: 'Maybe the labyrinth has no way out. There's nothing says it might – you just go round and round....'

'That is my view,' he says, 'But you needed to find that out yourself.'

'My dilemma – is not a labyrinth,' I say: 'The true maze is one built so you can get out of. Maybe not "you" but somebody. Don't be fooled – getting out, that is the goal. Reaching the middle, sitting lonely on the bench – that's part of the punishment ... the sentence, not the reward. The labyrinth must be a structure with an exit, but what I'm in is none of that.'

I say, 'I had an idea – I guess a play, a theatre – you have to show your character by using the simplest means – a hat, a slouch, a pansy in your mouth. I had a vision – our bully bosses: – you give them each a plaster arm, armoured fingers down to the ground, the steely fingernails – hardly lifted off the floor – and all distorted. One hand, the pistol grip, that skews the body, the spine bent into a "C" for crime ... Guys like me – enormous heads, so high they reach the lights, but tiny bodies, frail, limbs like tines of forks, with points that prod, no garnering, nothing picked up, archives, documents and photos lie like straw ... among the bones and carrion, until away with everything.'

'A ballet?' Buryat says: 'To me, there can't be dialogue: none possible in your predicament. A drama? You've never even seen a play, don't know how it works.

'Each takes its life from what precedes it, and sacrifices its existence to the past. There is no 'here and now', not even on the stage.

'And Anna? Would she have a part?'

'Splints,' I say: 'Two-by-fours, rough-cut, that drop and splinter ... bandages that flap, and those Greek actor's boots – that raise her up, so you can't reach. Then there's the women – big breasts and little heads – or turn about: flat bodies, heads made tall with wigs, like Marie Antoinette; Madame de Pomp, thinking of cleverness, of "subjects", enigmas posed and solved....'

'You don't think much of anyone,' says Buryat, not even querying. 'Me? Where am I?'

'You in your moleskins, a converted hunting suit – a steel-shod stick for keeping bores at bay,' I say. 'You'd comment. Don't. Stay well out of it.'

'Right,' he says: 'That's the masquerade. It won't avail. But – I have the answer for you all.

'Dead. You die, all of you. No one can touch you then, nor threaten. If you're the sort, you can blame yourselves, your lack of love for your poor bodies. It's of no consequence, no interest to anyone at all. Don't worry – being dead's the cure for you. The best. You'll see.'

'Documents? We can print those,' I say: 'Holes in the ground? Planting cadavers? We're experts. But – the lying still forever – no, none of us is ready for that. We dream and we remember. We'd bring a heavy slab of past, laid on the future, carved full of sentiments we'd not been allowed to have....'

'You could have had anything you wanted,' Buryat says: 'Death is not a punishment without a crime, it's where forever your fantasy roams and whines, 'It could have been quite different'. You don't believe it? That's too bad.

'What I suggest is false, don't fear. You'll live, or rather – you'll believe you are alive, feel life. Yu'll have to work out where you are and how to live there; who you are.'

'Do I need to have Anna with me?' I ask: 'It was an error, hooking her: instinct, or generosity? That's all gone by, played out by now.'

'Don't dwell on things,' says Buryat: 'I'm not a believer in all this stuff myself – confessions, pardon and contrition. But you're a credulous crew, you humans. Anna is yours. My advice? Stay clear of those satanic groups, the concerts with black smoke, burning of books, all that.

'When she can't take you any more, she'll let you go, and you'll go looking for another Anna all your life.

'After your death, there's a new life – except ... you don't know where. Will you have riches? No, it's not plausible. Maybe you'll be a minority, without a culture, no protection – a family, a clan that lives at your expense. All your effort goes to them.... Your past sins? Yes, wiped out. Like they would be anywhere, even in life. But you will find there's new ones, waiting, to be calculated.

'This is what you want, and it will save you, give you cover, a new drama where you can wave your arms and shout, like when it went so bad for you.'

'I'll miss you, Buryat,' I say.

'You won't,' he says: 'You just won't know.'

*

I think ... an island? Sharks in the lagoon? Keep them out – keep everybody out. Birds – yes, birds of every kind. No criminals unless it's us. No one higher up than me. Nothing too implausible to believe, to give us faith – maybe kismet, simple rules ... No miracles unless they're fun, no holy families straining credibility, no eternity, no creation with an intellect, a conscience; nothing that interrupts the hit and miss of evolution. No concerts.

'Would you want that, Anna?' I ask: 'Rebirth. Born again as something absolutely different?'

'Oh,' she says, 'I believe that. Not knowing who you've been. Like raising from the dead – I believe that, yes. I don't want it. I've no say in it. Reborn ... you wouldn't know, not anything, so there's no point.'

'Not remembering,' I say, 'It's not like not being. Some people take amnesia as a sickness. We would escape everything – like jumping from a burning 'plane. Arriving on the ground safe, blown through, without a memory.'

'No,' she says: 'I don't get on that 'plane.'

'It should please you,' I say: 'The chance of being someone, somewhere, else. The chance of having not a single memory, no pain, no pleasure, no resentment and no brakes.'

'Breaks?' she says: 'That's what happens if you have no brakes.' We laugh.

'It's still a cage,' she says.

'That's what the birds say,' I say, 'All over's always still a cage.'

'It's not the kind of life they would have chosen for themselves,' she says.

'We have the need to change,' I say: 'They don't. We have to escape, escape ourselves, a past. They don't. For them – life's just an ordinary confinement. They were given wings. Wings work, you leave – and then you make the journey back. Your destiny.

'We humans just invent it all ourselves.'

*

The river – it seems endless, you can be sitting in an upright chair, nothing special. Once invented, those chairs are found all over, like the cats and dogs – and you paddle with your hands, quite unavailing, and you keep your feet quite still in case you fall and are engulfed. It seems endless, the journey on the river, the river – *is* endless – it swells out into a sea, that seems to heave forever, then there is another mouth, another river, and up you go, it's harder work, and there are few of you, and you pass slow the people going past, down, quite fast, sitting terrified in their chairs, but moving easily, carried by the force....

'I'm peaceful now,' sys Anna, 'Quite tranquil. But you know – I don't understand you, and the contacts you have made. The plots, the intrigues – how you turn them into conversation, calculation. Don't press me, don't imagine all I see can make a story that gets better as it goes along. I am a horse, remember. I might be your horse, but horses are made so they can make a journey with anyone, anyone at all, and they can pull a dog-cart or a dray. I'll do anything you want, and anyone who wants can have me all – but: I'm a horse. That's what I am, to me it's good: to you – I am a horse. Don't expect me to answer you, to raise a point, to form a strategy, respond to your abstractions, laugh or cry with you, comfort you when you die, or ask for comfort when I die.'

'I understand,' I say, 'It's good you're tranquil, but it's not good news. I need a horse, for sure – there's no roads here, no settlements, no one to haul anything, so – good! You are my horse. But that's not what I need, I want. It's not a prejudice – the opposite. I love you, horses. You see almost everything, without a comment, but in your way, you see and calculate, you perceive. But between your eye and mine – there is a bridge that we can't cross.'

'A donkey's lighter,' Anna says: 'For sure, I'm not cute like them, and they have moments of a lightness I don't have. Beneath the toughness – they are sentimental, but you need to dig.'

*

This is the island. It makes no sense to wonder what you were before. You must survive, and find the means. Before this you were your father, and he died and you won't see him, never more.

Creation made the sea, the soil, the rocks – it didn't make the fish, nor you. You make yourselves, and they do too, those fish, your food. We living things, we come and go – nothing directed us, told us what to do – we invented all the stories, the rites, we guessed what we should and shouldn't do. No one told us anything at all.

'You're slow,' Anna says: 'I'd like you slower still – like those dragons on the beach, or a turtle. It means you learn slow, terribly slow, if you are one of those. When we are five, we know it all, we humans. It takes you, turtle, two hundred years, and you never ever don't do anything at all. And nothing, nothing with everything you know.'

'I used to be more active, yes,' I say: 'I was a robot. Full of stuff I knew. You must be very careful what you make, invent. I was very strong, stronger than a host of you. I could march all day, and knew what "justifying" meant. Doing bad when bad is done to you. Not just splitting words to fit them into oblongs, pages, but why some things are consequences and you can't question them. It's self-evident, even if you're stupid. So they say. Other things – aren't justified – but it makes no difference, none at all. It's evident, and yet – is anything self-evident ... Or – is it all?'

'You need do as little as is possible,' she says: 'As a robot, "doing" isn't really what you mean. "Think", "do", it's what you are, are made for. Doing is your planned limit, think is thinking within your bounds: what you do is what you can, decided – there's nothing novel. We lost those wasr, the battles we thought were decisive. And they were – win and lose, both; decisive ... Humans aren't made to do anything at all: just climb, eat, sleep. That's all.'

'You can't make a conversation, Anna,' I say, very irritated: 'You don't make sense.'

'There'll be an island,' she goes on, 'Where they all landed, a big boatload, and now it's populated with them, robots, all doing what they want. Outside the programme.'

'You see?' I shout, 'Nonsense. Misuse of thought and language.'

And if there is? That island? Robot island, in our archipelago. Evolution. Procreation. Ordering a 3D printer to make spare bits....

'All you need know, Anna,' I say: 'Is that these machines, robots – all they were supposed to serve was to eliminate the need – the instinct – to make slavery.'

'That, I never heard,' she says: 'And did it work? And were we slaves? Now?'

'Of course not,' I say.

'The howling,' she says: 'Like someone's warming up. It's preparing for something I fear and don't know what....'

'The Devil, Anna,' I tell her: 'There's other islands near. We hear them, they – would hear us if we made a sound. The devil is a metaphor – there's only one, it's everywhere. And if it sings?'

'I'm terrified,' she says.

'And so you should be, Anna,' I tell her: 'And if it swims? Or flies? There's sharks, always on patrol. They bear our hopes, they smile, help us maintain our distance. Will it hold? Be careful. Trust them? Don't risk, not anything, not ever.'

*

I don't eat the fish. First, it was sentiment, now – a principle. Principles don't need to mean that someone does the same for you. Besides – the algae's thick. It's choked the fish. If this was paradise – there'd be a means – a herbicide – to cope with all the algae. If paradise is garden, gardening, there will be pruning hooks and stuff you bind round trees to stop the ants. I live on plantains ... is it good for you? Maybe – a start. There's coconuts, and things, come floating in.

The rest of us ... they walk around: two by two, indifferent to all the other two's ... they climb the little hill where we'll all run to if the sea comes up ... They shout 'hoo-hoo – waaaahhh': their conversation.

You'd think they'd have opinions they would want to share, be part of the collective mind, its shuffling the cards, the rules. But no – they seem contented, knowing they're within the net, the being like the others, matched, mismatched ... By looking at them you can't tell the happy and the miserable, it's what you ought to know at once by sight, maybe they don't know what they are. Don't care. Stuck in it, whatever, irremediable.

You know the fates that probably they will escape; and one that certainly they've not.

Round and round and up and down – the youngest ones make scooters out of two planks, two cans. The family, its affiliates: – competing and collaborating, mostly there's no call to kill or maim. Is there a course, a track that everyone can follow, independently and reach ... the settlement, the streets, the lines of huts, the animals – if there were some – in pens, at rest?

Philosophy says they are my brothers, sisters – they don't seem like that. Philosophy was born of slavery, slave societies, and then the serfs, the servants. It died when wage labour prevailed. What's left? 'Be kind.' 'Be kind, or you'll lose lustre.'

What's next?

*

We're pale. Almost white. How is it possible, that we're ghosts?

'It's not uncommon,' says a guy, an acquaintance, who's full to brimming with the answers: 'Finish it off,' he says: 'Be really white, there's pipe-clay, and for contrast – black mud: pitch. All over – don't be shy.

'More drastic – you could paddle the whole show to where the heat is less. These little islands are a fake, they're military, floating boiler-plate, all surplus. Stable, our island, our foot-rest; it wallows. It stands on lids, hinged watertight to make an empty shell ... If you can force a path across the sea on foot – the algae are so dense – or pole and paddle, you'd move the whole caboose, the fake soils, the false bivalves, the archipelago, to where you want to be; out of the routes of warships.... But, it's just a cosmetic fix. Nothing will happen here – fault of the backlog.... No decision, no way out – unless....'

'It's the food' I say: 'We're many, and it's scarce: very scarce. We could eat each other, but it wouldn't last. If only everybody thought about it: – what we need, don't have.

'Those couples! They love the morning strolls, scanning the distances.... And the Shrine! Any trouble, they go, watch the show, new put on that morning; there's music all day long ... Relax! The prayer, it gives a tasty take on anything at all, just pop a pebble in the box. Your due.'

'Anna,' I say: 'There's the adventure. Risk everything, find a better place.'

'No,' she says, pulling a sour face: 'Here, it's ideal. I want to die here, where there's no sentiment, no person that I cling to, no past, no future. That way, life has no envelope, no covering, concealment. No address. You live it simple, crude, at its fixed pace – no cloud, no dust, no silk, no wool, nothing made by animals – nothing at all.

'There's nothing that says "stay", nothing to have you prefer uncertainty to the eternal dark.

'Let's have done with it, and not pretend we have complained and suffered merely as a pose, that really we preferred the awfulness to nothing – nothing whatever....'

I say, 'I thought you responded to the music, Anna, that it meant something particular to you, while we were jiggering about and smoking, leaving our skins behind....'

'No,' she says: 'You were mistaken.

'I wanted something special, extraordinary – but it turns out you're a human. Typical. You blame me for your mortality. Your weakness – it must come from me ... Instead, weakness is what makes humans pout and boast and long for being what? Strong?'

'We dream,' I say, 'Of other lives we had. Or – someone did? Or lives are maybe made of metaphors and pieces stuck on, haphazardly. We stretch them out, like gum – we say that's logic, act and consequence: – it isn't so. Everything is consequence, a scuttling from the danger or the stasis.... No logic, no act full of it. One thing leads to another thing, to strangenesses we must remember or we lose a crazy plot, the thread....'

'It doesn't change a thing, however it may be: the picture show that you call "life",' she says. 'Strange or not – it passes, there's no critic, tongue in cheek. Remember the old newsreels saying at the end – "take another look at life again soon...." That was the truth, leaked out....'

'And what of us?' I ask: 'Us two? Where does the dream, the stream – where does it take us, what's the picture? The Flight...?'

'I am indifferent,' she says: 'And yet, that isn't true, it's that I have no choice, no remedy. Whatever happens – I shall grieve, lament, regret. So, what you may do – for me, it's sad. Finish, that's all.'

'It seems to me,' I say, 'Yours is the only life there is. To you. For you, Anna, there is no context, what goes on impinges on you, but no one else. The others, they are not real and sentient like you. You could make your unique life magnificent – a strut, a preen, an epic of a hundred thousand lines. But you do not. You make it dull and insignificant ... Don't even think I have a fear, a reservation, about women – that would be an insult to us all. I love you, but you are not there. And so – I don't.'

'It's useless,' Anna says, 'You make catastrophe, try to escape. It's tough, but into more catastrophe you finish up....'

*

Flat-bottomed. That's what I need. Like in the Everglades, to skim across the weeds, driven by enormous fans. Leave Anna, look for no one else. No concerts, no moments and no spurs of moments when you introduce new characters, no oddities. You do not die, you stop, when the invention stops. In War and Peace, like the Frenchman says, 'You must be human, we're all mortal ...' and exits, disappears.

Is it hope, intelligence, despair, that makes me certain I must leave these hopeful, desperate people – strolling on their island?

Those noble penguins, couples with their son, their daughter, balanced on their feet ... an egg. How serious they look, and can't look any other way. I can try strutting, eggless.

There's no boat of the kind I need. The big lily pads – you cut two off and fix them so that you can walk, walk on the sea, the algae ... like snow shoes. You can even run, making circles with each step so's not to fall entangled ... ensnared, you'd fall on weeds....

Leaving everything behind, as it should be – as it will be for all of them.

*

I waddle on. I could be Rama, meeting the big monkey, Hanuman, making an alliance to find Sita – but no, it stinks here and the view is squalid. I've no one to make a deal with. Anna was not the type – too honest and too mean.

We always look for a new catastrophe, trying to have it work out right this time. My heart, my heart is not here, my heart's in the centre, far from the sea, far as can be ... Fallen empires, many, many of them, and no one left from them to blame or compliment.... the magnificence of the ruins.

'Don't head there,' says my future friend, poling contented on his plank: 'That's been abandoned.' He points far off, to a forest of tall trunks, some with green sprouts on their heads. Show-off money-towers in abandonment.

'It starts to sink,' he says, 'The roots take hold, and there's the tallest, stoutest trees you ever saw. Their day has come! They take over, ever stronger. The cement and glass drop off: – who knows, if there'll be fruit? A variety, maybe – what were the lower floors, festive with the ruddy pomegranate, then the peach, the quince above – and atop it all, the pineapple.'

'If you have come from there,' I say, 'The paradise, the *paradayada*, don't go to the archipelago, where I am from. Those Happy Isles are full of folk bewildered, since the happiness – it hasn't come, or doesn't last. They mope, grey souls. They seek. But I'm the only one to find a natural transport, that will take me out – ' and I wave a foot to show him how it's done – and fall into the weeds.

'Hey up, old hoss,' he says, pulling me out: 'My name is Solomon Crow. Here on the sea, we call ourselves whatever name we choose. No past, no clues, no reticence. It's hazardous – you could end up anywhere, so don't seek passengers. Improvise, rely on yourself, and don't take company.'

I suddenly feel weak, hopeless. I weep. He stares at me.

'You're odd,' he says: 'You're safe here, on your own, and you've escaped the worst. Be thankful. We're all single guys here, solitary, mature, there are no vengeful beasts, and our vendetta against nature has gone past. The hunt is over, done. Enjoy it, the windless calm.'

Don't crave land – you'll find sad people there, a host of them – why try to live life again, on land, with walking up and down and maybe exercising your dog?

'The good part is,' says Solomon, 'That no one asks you to pay bills. The less good – there's nothing here to buy or use. I'm sure they're working on it. But of course, despite the exhausting exercise, the rowing and paddling, environmentally we're in an excellent place; you don't feel hungry, or not much....'

Perhaps the air provides nutrition. They needed little at the start – fed by ravens, a jug of camel's milk, a twist of honey. The rustic roasts went to the gods – via the priests, their concubines. The rest lived frugal, raised the huge slabs and blocks of basalt, sandstone, without help, each toting immense weights, and dressing stone unaided ...

The times revolve, come round, the sea is flat, you skate – it's slick as a glass disc....

'We need to find more people,' I tell Solomon: 'Women. They can sort things out....'

'Bend your knees,' he shouts back, 'Don't be so stiff. You are a hinge, not part of the sea: – bend, sway! Women? They are princesses: probably you didn't take it into account. You messed up, grossly. Too bad, too late.

'We won't get help – we must solve things on our own....'

He's wrong. We see far off, some groups of people, some toying with their astrolabes, some shooting unseen stars: others in lines, busy with their Swedish drill.

'Don't go too near,' says Solomon: 'They look like they have it figured out. Science and exploration – finding a warm place in all the iciness, this present that goes on and on. There's no wall out there that forms a boundary ... the expeditions sally forth, are lost in the infinity.

'There's no need that we should work – it's all on automatic, and besides, out here there *is* no work. The resource – is weeds ... Those people' – and he gestures dismissively – 'Do nothing, so – nothing is what they are. What they watch and calculate – is only the passing of their time. Time. Is it eternal? What if it is? The future as our bodies knew it – has been invented. It will proceed, we won't. We have made freedom, and it seems a tragedy.'

'And was it not a tragedy before?' I ask: 'Think of the slavery, the battling, the struggle for the air, the water and the food? And for goods less useful – the myth, the epic, colour of the skin, the ugliness or symmetry; stuff of poetry, philosophy – all vanity. Vanity, dear Crow, dear Solomon – whoever placed me underneath your wing, your cloak.... Where shall we end ...?'

'Ah, poor dear,' he says, 'You need to keep your questions modest, close to your heart, your own precarious existence ... Where do we end? When? Beware – you seem to want replies that mean, perhaps, there can be "next", and "after" and "because"! I'm working on it. Those people ...' and again he gestures to the busy scientific, rationalist, crowd – 'Know they are dust from an immense quarry in the sky ... They know – "dust to dust", that it was all foretold, foreknown ... They're privileged – everything's laid out, already there. All you need do is – find the code. The mathematics – and it's done. You, poor fool – your object is your life and its environment – for which there is no code, no axiom. You are – ' and he laughs, pauses, 'All at sea.'

I sidle up to a group of them, as they pass round a paper, gesturing and hugging, some spitting in disagreement in the waves....

'Come away,' says Solomon, 'What have you got to give? They are indifferent to you. You can't be educated, still less programmed, to be of use to reason. Don't you see – the knowledge that they have, can't be passed on, there's no authority

to understand, enforce, nor yet to ignore, discoveries ...
Everything *ex nuovo*, and never conclusive. What can you add?
See, you can't stand on the ocean....'

And it's true. My feet are sinking in the sea. I step over, on to
Solomon's plank – we waver, nearly fall, the water reaches
ankles, then our knees ... 'Away, away!' he shouts. 'We must find
some firmer base! We cannot share: – these shards and splinters,
four by fours – they are made for one: – with two, they flounder,
swamp – they're overtopped by ripplets....'

'Dear Crow,' I shout, 'I cannot swim – besides, with all these
roots, I'd strangle anyway....

'Listen: I had in mind, since I can't be explorer, discoverer –
to conjure up a thought that changes lives at once – forever. Help
me, with the formula, to project my essence, leave my mark....'

'Yes,' he says, decisively: 'Changing the lives of all who hear.
Shout! Loud as you can! Yes, that is a worthwhile aim,
irrespective, naturally, of any value your messages might have.
Change, move it along – that is the best there is.

'The past ones – even bearing seals of sacredness – they made
their "POP", though they're with us, among us, still. But all they
do is serve the interests of the minute, the exhortations to your
side and 'screw whoever can't believe' ... Love and forgiveness,
tolerance – stay clear of those. They're stale and tired – slogans
for the bosses, the frosting on the poisoned cake....'

'I thought,' I say, 'That when, despite it all, you have a time of
happiness, however short, when you can say, 'yes, I'm happy' –
then, at that moment, you must leave. Run, escape, leave –
wherever you have settled, leave everything that makes you
pleased, or glad, or full of hope, forgiveness, understanding.

'Each happy time you leave, you have the memory, the
knowledge that whatever happens – *that* time, showed you could
be happy, and that you shouldn't wait for things to sour, for
deaths, abandonments, or kismet.... for anything to change....'

'And then you reflected....' says Solomon Crow....

'And thought "what rubbish, Solomon,"' I say.

'Instead, the wars you didn't want, the revolutions that you might have welcomed, maybe – none would bring happiness, quite the reverse,' he says: 'And try to work a message out of that!'

*

'Suppose,' he says, 'We could float for ever on this sea. Never thirsty, though we can't drink; and never sick – there's no movement, no infection – or rather, the infection's us, so we're immune. We are the pathogen, at sea amidst the other pathogens, the viral soup. Immortal, or at least, reprieved from disappearance, since we're the only ones alive, and visible ... in movement from here to there and back again. There is no happiness, and yet – there is enough time passed through that we can't say we are unhappy, or even miserable, or sad. And – there's no war, no revolution, just the groups of earnest honest searchers after knowledge that we come across – indifferent to us, seeking the beauty or the flaw that makes them thankful for another day of life, or fearful that they, and we, can't be sure if life it is ...

'But guys like us – we've no idea. We don't have the techniques, the theories, we don't know what an axiom is; equations, we did those at school and all they do is show one side is equal to the other one ... And that's my province of significance, dear friend – I am the expert, for whom an "a" is always equal to a "b", if you can shift the figures round, from side to side and like the conjurer – you show the empty hat is really home to doves, a rabbit ... show that life and void are much the same, that magic can be made with cards, a watch, a stooge's wallet – or a sword, thrust through an empty box....'

'Ribbons from your mouth ...' I say, joining in his fun: 'You are quite right. We've run out of messages – I can say that even magic is restricted to the trouser pocket, or the hat.'

*

Magic – where does it come from, where does it go? What is it
for?

'Leave out the last,' I say: 'Let's ask – illusion. Is that sleight
of hand, or – shall we wonder, and assert – "we cling to reality,
that's always moving. If it's not illusion, surely I can find a stretch
of grass, lie down on it, relax?"'

'You could ask, where does anything come from? Ideas, sperm,
fruit – and reality that always changes and yet we're told to cling
to it, shape it, frame it, hear its beat....' says Solomon.

'Any idiot can answer questions with a question,' I say:
'Unanswerable questions – those are the province of the idiots.'

I want to stretch out on firm ground.

'There's marsh,' says Solomon, 'And ice mountains – round
about.'

'It can't be so,' I say: 'Invention must create pillars driven in
the core, supports and floors. A platform will be made and earth
laid on. Instead of rock and sand and mud – you tip on stuff that
finds its rock, lies on it, its bed, like I would upon the earth. And
watch the sky.'

'The hardness, solidity? You're sure it must be close,
attainable' he says: 'Suppose – it would be very far away. And
penetrating, you might pierce the shell of soil and hit the fire
beneath. But, I suppose, you'd ask – what is distance? We can't
reach yesterday, not even that – but the world is small, we can
walk round the solid parts in years. Ten years – you'd get a long
long way. Far, far, afar, on foot, you can go round the peaks, the
lakes, and hope there are no soldiers in the way.'

Following his thread, I say, 'The distance – between your brain
and mine – in terms of heads: a metre. In terms of understanding
– the distance may be infinite, but anyway – immeasurable. I write
the message, send to you, and what you do has nothing at all to do
with me. Assimilating, internalising, grasping – debate,

elaboration – all that "communication" must imply ... a distance planetary ... or, just incalculable.'

'Ah yes,' he says, and laughs: 'The message. On the postcard. What mobilises you, makes up the army, determines the campaign, creates the lives and deaths; – and you, who sent it – you don't even lick the stamp.

'It's ratatouille and Chablis for you, as always, at midday. For me, recipient: – cold sweat, the fear and trembling, and maybe moral outrage.'

'People,' I say, 'Yes, we have to deal with them. Where are they, where have they gone, it must matter, especially to them, but how do we represent the mass? There's so many, some are so different, others indistinguishable ... millions. Almost all the languages you don't speak, and as for successful, ultimately failing, lives – who knows? In terms of village life ... it's moot. People have fifty goats, and next year – five. Not their fault. It is the cycle. So, you'll say, is life. Life – is goats, and then *a* goat.'

'Suppose most of them is dead?' asks Solomon, 'People.'

'They are put in fictions,' I say: 'Some, the dull ones, into books. The livelier into opera, on the stage. The dead – they fit in anywhere – in choirs, in groups, behind the camera. Sat in chairs or propped against the scenery, the descriptions of themselves stencilled on the walls.'

'But, they can't speak,' says Solomon, quite fascinated.

'Not a sound,' I say: 'That's one piece of common sense, of common knowledge – not a sound, no word. No one ever heard of dead people who can talk, but of course – they cannot disappear. They're everywhere, and so is what they built, the swords they made, the tank-shells filled, iron rations packed – and all the rest.'

'Postcards despatched ...' adds Solomon, contented. 'That solves the mysteries of where they go, have gone, without a fiddly counting those that's here, not here, and people you will never meet. In fact, it makes the two of us a sample, and dispels all doubt. There's life, existence – it only takes a single one to make it clear. That's all there ever is – all dangles from the brain of "one". And you're my witness, my accomplice. We happen to be alive, but it would be exactly similar if we were dead, so long as somewhere, someone carries on. A pair of eyes, or even just the one, can guarantee the universe is there, however much it dithers and goes dark.'

We laugh. 'You're a good sport, Solomon,' I say, leaning forward, clapping him on his bony back.

'Let's be off and find more people, if there are ...' he says, digging his pole between the water-lilies with great panache, and making speed. 'They'll be your choice. What you make of them.'

'There's been catastrophe here,' I say, 'And yet you give your time to help me out....'

'Time?' he wonders: 'I usually don't put it in a measure. There's so many ways you pass it, live it, see how it has unrolled, but time, I think, is homogeneous. Maybe it's not; in any case, there's memory. *That* is the time we live by, or the sensitive ones do, at least. You are a sensitive type, and there's not many like you, indeed, not many of *any* kind at all. But you might make a judgement, write it up: – my part. My counsels. Convincing fictions ... attributed: my name in golden letters... Fiction's all about the author anyway, but travestied – anyhow, her imagination is the source. Now, it's become an open secret, a tale about yourself; even the apartment numbers and the streets are as they are in someone's real.'

'Write? Your legacy?' I ask, taken aback: 'As you, as if I'm you? Or who? Would I need to make my peace with style – with formalism and with realism as well? Pondering a judgment, and about a breathing person too, that might, just might, be read for evermore?

'I have no past preparing me for anything like that. The *nouveau roman* – it aged and died while I was doing other things,' I say, thinking, rowing back, retreating.

'No matter,' Solomon says: 'Nothing was – nor ever is – resolved. Forgotten, changed – that's all. Enough that you were here that long that you remember what I say. That way, you are my rock, full of fossils from way back.'

I don't respond.

'You fear the nothing that comes after this,' he says, apparently amused, 'Afraid that what there is, right now, is nothing ... already nothing. Like the past and the future both – are nothing?'

'That's probably it,' I say, anxious to be away, not writing Solomon's life. What could it be worth?

'Afraid?' he asks, 'That's cute.'

I'm one of those who is convinced, that compared with something, the something that you know is at your fingertips, 'nothing' is what you have to fear....

'A paradox,' he shouts, 'You fear nothing!'

'You don't understand, it seems,' I say.

'Maybe I misjudged you,' he says: 'Maybe you're another irritating bug that can't connect with me....'

'We're all we have,' I say, 'Each other. Yet – no one will admit it, no one wants to belong to anyone! Let's not argue about what you are, and how I can't be your biographer, not knowing you, your aims....'

'My goal? To let the world remember me,' he says, 'Even if the world becomes much smaller than myself, my name.'

'Forget it, please,' I say.

He's poling off, fast and faster still.

I'm irritated, such stupidity. Anger:– along with fear, it turns the world.

I was rash, perhaps. I should have helped – even made a sacrifice. Solomon, who promised nothing, had sustained me. We didn't fit. I'm lost again, I have no fault.

I can't go back – there's no direction here to anywhere. How long did I float with Solomon, losing the trace, then finding it was him, the mission, and my task? Stuff I can't do, don't want.

He had no commitment, took no side. I wanted people to mix with, listen to – but he was the only one available for both of us.

*

Here's a long stave – poling with it, you go faster than walking, but the bottom yields, sucks at you – vegetation, logs, plastic, mud. There is no bottom, there's resistance. All mashed. And little islands – smashed. Blown up or blasted down?

Moria. The word remembered at the moment the tell-tale scenes appear. The sudden mass-deaths of fish, men, otters, flies. The human cadavers made smooth by water, the hair washed out. My brothers. Lumps of fat in the cold soup. Certainly guilty – of this or that, the bombing or the running, offense, defence, the shielding from the light and heat: – faces, soon worn down, flattened, roundels of sucked white, brown, of fudge.

So, that's where they went down, in the water. Leave it! People once ... enough, they had their day, don't think to start again....

Avoid the little whirlpools – down the frail rafts go, the empty fragile improvised craft – the teetering boxes, planks and fronds – down it all goes, theories too, for sure, 'culture', and its production, all sucked down.

Calm, all is calm, and natural – nature like it is, indifferent. Not beautiful, not kind or inspirational – not there to serve ... not there to kill and eat, be eaten: just duration. A million years of dust and rock, heat and ice....

Calm and natural, like I'm in a stomach decomposing, foul waters, stinky gases – in the end dried out, turned into peat or *tufo*.

Facts and values reconciled, no profit and no prophets, not in anything. All is nowhere. No eye to see.

See, invent – as if seeing were not always an invention: – billows, small children, running through the shallows, then on to decking, plunging, disappearing and up they come again, clambering for a foothold, racing along, arms waving.... My classmates? The little girls, treacherous and snippy, the boys violent, and flatulent. I gave them love, I thought. Those who had love wanted no more of it. Unrecognisable to those without ... There they go ... puzzles I have never solved – 'be a friend, a companion, make us laugh ... don't cry, don't fight back, don't take it serious, don't cling, now go away'....

No, it can't be them, they've long ago dispersed, fallen into other lives, into the fly-traps, the closed wards, the sunny upland pastures ... just blurs, sacks of wind and mist, blown along....

Leave them behind. In front – there is the ocean. No one, no one at all, not visible, no voices, no ships, no rafts.

The sea is the mirror in which you only see yourself.

Sea a hand-span deep.

And is there splendour here, in that? In us?

Intelligence. Use that. If there's a sea, there is a shore. It works that way.

The people – like the other lot, except – this time I'm ready.

I'm born. A wise small baby.

'I need protection and love,' I say.

'Can you pay?' she asks: 'You might consider marrying me in time, or I could find you a boyfriend? Then there's children....'

Mother? Sister, ex, estranged – searching for love, love lost.

'I'll think about it,' I say: 'But of course, I'll pay.'

Here we go, here we go again. This lady, generous, perhaps from a story-book for kids ... and am I still the same one she'll decide she didn't like?

We could live here till we're very old, lost our minds and can't put on our clothes without some help.

The little house is on the river-bank, so if you grow up quick, you'll see the spates, but maybe you'll avoid the monster floods. The best part is the cats and dogs; I love them, and when they die, into the river they can go, away, away, turning over like tumbleweed, and then they're gone, for good, and you remember every one with pleasure undiminishing.

People. I never mastered them – 'putting on a different face' ... 'putting a different face on things ...' Where did all those old faces go, why did they risk losing them, where did all the faces come from, and the loss, when it always comes, is what? – of self? Of selves? People who'd pretend to be somebody else, not a someone born and breathing, but just – another person, identical, but different...

If one thing's strange, then all are strange.

The splendour of the species, its pretence, pretensions, and the disasters it had caused.... If only – it had never tried, never gone on its ramp, its rampage, and ruined everything and everyone.

All forced, enticed to be thieves, assassins, liars, greedy, dirty parasites ... Accursed, damned, bringers of disaster, blind, insensible until – still protesting, still reasoning – we frizzled up like slugs and snails: in the burning oven, on the hot flat stone.

A mistake? A destiny? A future graphic in the mind? Stop, change ...! But there it came. The future's coming so you can be alive in it.

This place – I'm sure the people here are organised; they're standing round, quite orderly and quiet. Probably there's no resources each could own – there's trees not bearing fruit, slender, the buildings botched and patched. Everyone responsible for their own accomplishments and gifts, no private wealth, no communal ease – a place where I'd need counsel, who to trust, how to survive not prospering but not degrading. Women? Men? Seek out someone, a category, eccentrics, the isolates? A partner, or a confidant, stimulus or cautionary?

My cradle.

*

I step towards them, my legs are long and powerful now: all new and different. The place has grown, it seems – and yet, it cannot be. The world is what there is, no copy can exist, *I*'ve grown, I've aged. That's all. The world accommodates, keeps on enfolding me, like skin.

'You're a persistent type,' says the woman who first spoke to me, detaching from a lively group: 'That would suit me, suit just fine.' She's like the other ones – they're like oysters – one in a thousand has a pearl, one in a million a pearl that you can sell.

'There's nothing special, wanting to survive,' I say: 'But I'm most grateful – I need friends, intimates, a life scaled up and down on them – as if they're keys on the piano; some black, those are the in-between, the sceptical, the more precise, but necessary....

'Although, I feel a person needs to know what he or she is for, what life's about, before you set about making your own, carving it out....'

'Like worn-out ordinary stuff, pieces without particular prices that you try to sell – in the market where the refugees hang out,' she says, amused.

'I'm not a refugee,' I say: 'I didn't expect to find a refuge. I'm a traveller. I grow. Without hope, but curious.'

Does she offer, want, affection? Sharing of projects, secrets, puzzles?

'No,' she interrupts my thoughts, 'I have people, other trusted people, who serve for those, the more involving themes. I think everybody has, or ought to have, a host of specialists, of friends who cover everything, all happenstance. They alert you with the action-words – "go easy on the camel, your friend; his back".'

It's true. I feel her saying this prefigures loss, an anticipation of a loss for me. She's put together something whole. Is there a space left I can fill?

'I hope you've nothing against black,' she says, 'The in-between piano keys.'

'Lili', says a pin on her lapel. She's black, but a piano doesn't work like that....

'This is not a state, a country, nor a culture or a place where each stands up for somewhere they come from, or feel is special to them,' she says. 'The same with colour, height and girth – and all of those combined!' She laughs, some of her group join in.

'Look,' she says, holding out a folder: 'Say what you think.'

It's labelled '*Rabot* and robots ... After work – who whom?'

'If we don't work, there's no more social class, perhaps.' I say: 'But if the robots aren't the bosses, someone else is, that's for sure.'

'If you've riches, you don't work,' Lili says. 'So, the robots can't touch you – you're immune. You'll be the cleverest, it's clear, paying to invent the robots that make everybody idle, no longer pestering, and greedy too.'

'I'm not sure ...' I say: I don't like the way Lili is putting things, but – prudence: 'I haven't read the argument, I'm afraid.'

'We're in good hands,' she says: 'The robots work out problems, make our futures beneficial and secure. It's a great relief, a blessing for us all.'

'My journey,' I say, 'I didn't see them, robots, nor rich. No one helped me – but I'm here.'

It's true. There's nothing more to add.

Except ... I say, 'Those protectors, if you have them, if they exist and are as benevolent as you would wish – suppose they put protecting you above all else? Might your robots fight the others, just for you?'

'Oh no,' she says, 'We discuss. We're not deluded. Besides, the robots are immortal, or nearly so. They can learn and be improved, don't have the limits that we do.'

'I'm sure you're right to honour them,' I say. 'Obeying too, if you are sure they take you into account, foresee what they're not planned to do, and don't react in hurtful ways.'

'Up to a point,' says Lili, looking askance at me, and pushing me out of the circle of her friends. 'We have the faith. We must.'

'And if they say that you must fight?' I ask.

'There is free will, of course,' she says: 'Philosophy....'

'There's no philosophy that's free of the objections of another one,' I say, '*A priori* in its process, flawed in language, observation of reality. You choose the least bad, the one that's closest to your interests or your convictions. Your robots are the same, unless you've left philosophy out of them....'

'Let's talk of something else,' she says: 'We're happy now, fulfilled and confident.'

She shares me with the other ones – those friends, acquaintances, more fun, more sexy, creative or inspired. She's very patient – she accepts them, poets who re-write for ever, gamblers, prospectors of all kinds ... I'm like I said, a traveller. My experiences unverified, unverifiable – and I'm tired, sick too – big ulcers on my thighs, all-over plaques of mottled skin from toxic water, kidneys like rubber balls.

There's often talk of brain studies, of the 'evolutionary path', and I jump in – 'forget it', I say,

'I want none of that,' and so the subject's dropped, but not, I'm sure, abandoned.

It reminds them – I came in by chance, my origin, development unknown. Not one of them, a stranger, or probably just strange.

'You keep so quiet,' says Lili: 'That means you're stupid, or you've a vision of the world so big – it's got so big, it's you!'

She laughs, and friends – hers, mine – they gather round.

'I'll start with the Creation, and our favoured birth – dust or stardust, there on our upward ramp, right from the Light,' I begin: 'You see – we're made of residues, off-cuts of the universe, unforgettable and unforgot – an epic, which, if you reach the end – achieves Nirvana: comfort, destiny, salvation. But – that is the art, the inspiration: – the poetry of hope. Instead – the wars, the contests for the favoured space – Peoples of God! All of them: favourites of the divine, no sacrifice too great, no martyrdom eschewed – and then, with duty done: Messiah. Peace and love. All lies....'

'Oh no,' she interrupts. 'Not chiliasm too!.... Don't say that it's all lies ... all except your own....'

'Inventions, Lili,' I say, incautious and plumped up.... 'The only pursuit that beats the lies, the eternal jousting to reach the top, to win the tokens, take the food – the only way to challenge lies requires your cash. Lots, is best. That's not lies, it's real ... although, although....'

'Inflates, deflates, is taxed and fined and cheated on ...' says Lili: 'Go on. Let all your madness out, and hope it won't infect us all....'

'Destruction, penury – the failure to control the damage we have made,' I say, 'That starts to weigh. The journey, the commitment, palls. What next? Creation of a new creator – one we have made ourselves, with all our skills: machines. They'll win their independence, take direction of our destiny, shoulder the sadness and the disappointment – oh Lili,' and I weep, 'Lili, you don't feel the tragedy. Stuck on this reluctant, temperamental rock ... To you, pacific people camping here, it's what you have: surrender, zilch. A benediction, food trucked in from who knows where, for what....'

'I'm sure we earned it,' Lili says –

'Of course you did,' I say: 'And when you have to pay, you'll see the price is your recruitment – into what, I cannot say, but be sure, it won't be easy, and the pain immense.

'Another scene? What they have promised, over time – and never comes. Useless to list what you'll not have....'

'That's it?' asks Lili: 'All? Finished so soon? Most people who're disturbed like you go on and on....'

'I'm sad, I've had enough,' I say: 'We all must suffer; those who cheat and those who're conned. There are no discounts, all depends – '

'On how you spin the wheel,' she says.

'No, no,' I say, alarmed: 'Beware! The victims, the most pitiable, are the hopeful ones who thought that every spin would have them win ... immunity ... a preferential path, no obstacles....'

How can they escape? ... these people, designated by themselves as losers, excellently so. Avoiding war: – defence the same as preparing for attack, and so they've no intention to defend.

'You'll always live beneath the threat,' I say, 'The fear, the punishment for crime, the vengeance, the punishment from criminals....'

'You should trust more,' she says: 'We're not ingenuous.'

'That is the least,' I say: 'The minimum. Be suspicious! ... As if intelligence could steer your path through life. Remember, from the start, life drops you naked, impotent, defenceless: a stranger feeding you, surrounded forever by more strangers ... Who will defend against the malevolent, and the indifferent? However strong or pliable you are – they will be waiting for you....'

'We thought of that;' she says: 'You must have nothing to be envied for.'

'The secret formula? That, in itself, is enough to make you all desirable,' I say. 'Tranquillity, and stasis? It makes you targets.'

'We're early peoples now,' says Lili: 'Like the people they called barbarians – who fought with bows against the cannons and machine guns: the colonised, and the enslaved. It wasn't intelligence that had them beaten into slaves – just their inventiveness. With us – our resource is the intelligence. It's universal. Everybody has it, in the quantity they choose. The guys that boss us – they're not smart, but they create intelligence, and so are well-equipped. They use the intelligence they've acquired. We don't oppose, and don't resist. We're smart. We don't want robot wars.

'The new intelligence is made to beat you down, and take your goods, your riches. If you don't have them – perhaps, you will be safe. Safe and enslaved. But they – don't have imagination, don't have fantasy and specially – they don't have Dada, that is still with us.'

'I don't see any sign of it,' I say.

It's true. They talk and read, but nothing you'd call fantasy, a challenge to what's observable and necessary. No Dada; no Dodo.

'Obviously,' Lili says: 'Anything you prize – you cannot show. It's locked away. If not – it's stolen, probably traduced.'

'I'd never thought of it like that,' I say: 'I come from far away, a journey hard, where every wave requires your concentration ... no time for flights of fancy....'

'You can't look up, I understand,' she says: '... look up and see the birds, and take your lesson from them. Sing, fly. You must stare down – just fish and snakes and eels: – the workaday, the shadows, gliding, twisting, underneath your feet, your paddle....'

'I understand the danger, Lili,' I say, 'Greater intelligences, that push us off the mountain top. But they're banal.'

'We don't have personalities, nor character,' she says: 'That's why we're not creative. We lost our qualities along the way. The ancients didn't have them either – they saw how you dressed, what fabrics cost, and jewels – but all that mattered was your caste, your status: slave or free. The rest was all invented later; then it too went. It was of no consequence.'

'Lentils and rice – I enjoy the diet,' I tell Lili: 'No fuss, it's just trucked in – some would find it monotonous, but they'd find life a bore and death still worse ... The diet? You're smart if it protects you against catastrophe. It saves you work and thought – but is it a sign of your intelligence, that whoever sends the trucks, can satisfy you with so little, and receive – what, in return?

'After all, animals who can't do sums assert their particularity – the porcupine, the aardvark – they have their characteristics, they're characterful, clear outlines and specialities ... they soldier on, they're hunted, poisoned, killed by autos – but....'

'That's their adventure,' Lili says, quite prim: 'Leave them to it, us to ours.'

'... People too,' I insist, 'They must have some qualities – a roar, a purr. Even a furry skin that makes a scarf: a grin, a trick. Let them indoors, clear up their mess – they'll surely reward with gratitude....'

'Listen,' Lili cuts me short: 'We enjoy it here. Better could mean worse, it always does. You – however many lives you have, you'd not like any of them. Escape and suffering – that's your path.

'Time. Try to understand it – what is stone, and what is water. What is eternal shade, and how to reach the light. What is looking at you, what's attacking, and what is running....'

'The deer, the tiger and the hare?' I ask. 'The dancing toad – I love that! The stone – the sound that travels round the circle, dies, is heard far off.... a signal, words ...

'All metaphor, a contemplation and a poetry....'

'Oh,' Lili says, 'It doesn't take so long to grasp, I'm sure. You have to keep things simple, like we do. Not complicated, like you do.'

'I sought you, Lili,' I say, 'But maybe you weren't lost.'

'You're desperate,' she says: 'It's a turn-off. Strong emotion's like raw booze – it kills the liver. Act cool. Find a place that's good, people will have settled there.'

*

They live here in small beach huts – like tourist havens; mock thatch, sand floors. It used to be a 'colony', for people who'd forgotten what that signified. Bad food and watered drinks: and sex, promised, postponed.

'Lili,' I tell her, 'You're soft outside and hard inside. Being soft makes you gullible, and being hard means you put up with life....'

'Just tell me,' Lili says, 'Why I should be friends with you. Your qualities? A theory you've elaborated – that should be heavy, new? Theory of everything, or something big at least. If you've no material that's useful to me, you're a net loss, but let's pass on – are you delightful? Sexy? Entertaining or informed? A handyman, a fourth at bridge, musician, someone who identifies the movie stars that we've forgot? Do you have contacts – life-changers?'

'I try,' I say. 'But in the end, you're right: I'm average or just below in almost everything.'

'Life? Destiny? The future? Do you have a special take?' she asks: 'Or follow the bellwether, like the rest? Are you an original?'

'Friends mostly aren't,' I say: 'For the average or just below – there are their average friends; friends kept for what they are, simple and naked, drifting timorous through life... Or else – they're conmen, robbers, exploitative tarts – hoodlums and fraudsters ... those are friends as well, and you must bear with them or evade ... terrorists and hunters, narks and liars, foolish, perverse – who lust after your imagined wealth, your body or your credit....'

'Exactly,' Lili says: 'This is the modest place where all these negatives don't stick. The question here is – "what are your precious gifts", not "what's your covert scheme?"'

'That is too bad,' I say: 'I'm an expert in the 'covert scheme'. I spot resources, or a place to dig, at least. It's a sense inherited, I guess – living in forests, possibly.'

'I told you,' Lili says, backing off and looking worried: 'We must have almost nothing ... no wealth, no hidden treasures, no skills. Already there's the tribute to be paid....'

'No,' I say, 'All that I see here – you're undistinguished. Talentless. For you, that is a good. You discuss what others write and think – and that is all. You're courtiers without an oath, a loyalty ... no prophecy, no mission.

'But – what is this "tribute" that you pay?'

'People, young people,' Lili says, low and respectful, 'Get sent off. A quota. Almost everybody, and they don't come back. Slaves, soldiers? Settlers? People like me – they pass us over. Or we arrive as adults from some other place....'

'What's wrong with you, Lili?' I ask, rude and curious.

'It's the food,' she says, and opens her robe, flashes – a thin discoloured body, hanging on a central ridge of bone, the kneeless legs set off, suspended from the outside edges of a wide pelvic bridge – the tiny genitals – then she closes the curtain, ends the horror show...

'I'd no idea ...' I begin, taken far aback. 'What does the tribute mean?'

'Service,' she says: 'Service before everything. We're told.'

'So?' I ask.

'I can't do stairs,' she says: 'Here, there are none. There – it's normal, I presume.'

I'm ashamed of being shocked. It shows ...

'You're not a good person,' she tells me: 'You're rubbish, arid. It's no consolation. Quite the reverse.'

It's an opinion. I press on, 'So, you were dumped here,' I say: 'Because of war? Or peace? Or some distress ... Food? That becomes consequence, not a cause....'

'We all are dumped. It's birth; among strangers in strange lands' she says: 'The important part is trying to escape what is inevitable....'

'And have some fun,' I say: 'That's what's always been left out....'

'You've always known it's hard,' she says: 'You could try acting on it, what you know: ... the penury, amassing of scarce stuff....'

'I've been on the water,' I object: 'Staying afloat. Alone.'

'Are you sure,' she asks, 'It's other people that you want?'

'Other people,' I say: 'You need them to protect you from the other people.'

'I might have helped,' she says: 'Until you started speaking. Here, we all talk a lot, we have our plans, we paint and rhyme and think of quips. You – you've just explored. Is this the place you want to be, what can you have it do for you, what is it proof against ...?'

'Not war, for sure,' I say, 'Or pestilence. The water's rising too – if it continues, we'll all be moving on.'

'Don't worry,' she says: 'We've had world wars. Nowhere is touched the same, some places hardly at all. You know it's everywhere, but it's also different everywhere, and you survive. The world? Enmities? No one seems to want all that to end, even if that were the goal ... there is an indeterminacy, complicity, hedging of bets ... All the world's peoples, however they line up, fight to the death, they die, and yet – some will survive and multiply. Over and over. Each time the end must be the end, you think, and yet ... it never is. You must have hope for that....'

'Hope?' I cut in.

'You don't want to suffer more and longer?' she asks: 'Surely not. Prison may drive you crazy – but not so's you want execution. Maybe you can't bear to live on in your cell, but it is home....'

'That's true,' I say: 'We want fun, but not to lose our little space, unless it's for a smaller, more protected one.'

'You won't find that,' says Lili, decidedly: 'You're the sort others want to see moved on ... You're special, if that consoles you – you are distinctive. Abrupt, convinced, impatient. Even inventive, for yourself ... You are a battered battle tank – dedicated to escape. No other thought.'

'I'd hoped to find in you,' I start, and think of how small, uninhabitable, that body seems, the shaky gimcrack trestle that kept her vertical ... lodged, supported ... Not just evasion, something different....

'They go on fighting,' she says, 'Until you think they want to kill them all, the enemy, and then they stop. Then they think of something else. Domination, humiliation.'

'It's because we're smart,' I say, and we laugh.

'You must be missing something,' she says: 'Some conviction, passion, faith. Everybody has the drive to win – you don't. You're a rebel, and you rebel against your own rebellion. Useless. Just to survive, move on.'

The water's rising. Lili can't do stairs – there's no stairs here.

Tall marsh birds. This is their paradise, they'd never move, there is no better place – and then – whoosh. They decide, they're gone. Prevision, or indifference?

'It's river water,' Lili says: 'The leaves, petals ... like buttercups ... A dam, a weir, broken open....

'It's liberated. While we all have life-sentences, locked in.'

'It couldn't know,' I say, 'Don't envy it, the river.'

Fire and smoke lit from below – volcanoes, everybody says – the whole horizon blazes with them, as if the limit's broken – first the river, then the earth break out; grey spots of stickiness and stink, on your face and neck like scars and smokiness you must carry round. Volcanoes in the sea.

'Making happy islands,' Lili says, 'Making land with hills.'

It looks like, yes, perhaps: volcanoes....

'More land,' I say, vaguely, weakly: 'You know, when I met Solomon Crow, I fell, I drowned. I was sure. Land's what you need, or you go down, you die. Land – for the birds to rest, for the lemons to grow on. Maybe, Lili, if you'd had lemons to eat, your body would have looked in better shape.'

'Don't patronise,' she says: 'All this water – it's thinned out the crust, the crust of soil, that keeps the fire from breaking out.'

'The lava,' I say: 'It could save us all. It's fertile – black soil, like they have in Russia.'

'You invent,' she says: 'That does no harm. For you, there's life immortal, everywhere, over and over. Bite or fawn, that's what you say, for you, the human enterprise is all contained in that....'

'A dog's existence,' I say, trying to make her smile.

'A good, a useful life,' she says, 'You don't know what that might be?'

'No,' I say: 'You have to try – every angle, keep on poling, hoping the stick will find a solid base and give you traction. That's it. Meeting the people but taking yourself away, not having them take slices off you – although you know – they mostly do.'

'You're grimy,' Lili says, amused: 'You've leant against some dirty walls, been rolling on the floor of doorless huts. You ought to meet the Noisy Crew – they talk a lot about a flight, far far away from here. They write long manifestoes, perform concerts of brute Noise – they steal, they lie, they love their failures, tell us we're the foolish ones to undervalue creativity – everything, they say, is to be done, admired – for its own sake. No rules. All that is, is brought into existence, is valuable, to be admired; above all – not to be repeated, copied. No striving for originality – the unique is within the core of everyone, innate, and that is all you need... The act, the deed, spontaneous and committing – do nothing that another person does, has done ...

'It's crime, I think, disturbs, unsettles what they say. We're on the edge, here on this marsh, and anything that's different is disastrous, it wobbles us ... instead of a renewal, the *style outré* falls sick, impoverished, makes us ship more water to excess, sink below the line ... The crime they welcome blows them all away, itself as well.'

'That's what they always say,' I say: 'That Dada's just like Disco – lounge around and watch it die. It always threatens to destroy what is, and open the horizon to infinity. They say it's just a phase, a style, a rhetoric.

'As for crime – that's always new, it hopes; tries to be unpredictable, and yet the motivation's always identical, and crude ...'

Lili smiles. 'It's you,' she says: 'Don't do your pious act. You'll like them for a while, the Crew.'

*

The Crew sits around making their noisy instruments, painting very noisy pictures. The women are the most expert.

There is dead quiet.

I tell them who I am, my name.

'It's of no interest,' says the tall lady: 'What does "Hugo" or "Brittany" tell us? Be who you like – it's not of concern to anyone but you. And even you will want to think, to change, or not to think, to change....'

'You really don't have anything,' I say: 'Except the noise. And now – there's none even of that. Not a rustle, just sometimes a rasping and a swish of hairy sticks on dried-out leaves....'

'Right,' she says: 'Nothing. Just noise and silence. We decide – it makes no difference, except it's *our* noise, our silence.'

'It's very basic,' I say: 'Very thorough. I'm like you, a *Neinsager.*'

'Yes and no,' she says: 'There's nothing here to recognise, nothing to change, so everything's not here.'

'True,' I say: 'Everything can be changed, does change, so if there's something that does not, that you can't alter – it can't be here.'

She screams, right in my ear: '*We* change, all the time, all we want. We leave, all the time: – we've left. Listen to me, the sound of the storm, the silence of air in a bottle, in a tire.'

'You know,' I say, 'You're much too articulate for me. It all makes sense, too much ... the sense that nothing else round here does....'

'Here? What's here and what is there?' she asks, a fine Jesuit! 'When you're here it's here, and when you're not, it's there. Where is the difference?'

'I'd leave with you,' I say, 'But not to stay. You're much too rational for me. You'll undermine the tribute, you're the young ones who resist....'

'In each of us,' she says, 'There is an old old person, waiting to decay and fall – the rotten apple, too long on the branch. A fruit of what? Good and bad? You wouldn't eat it. I told you, it's putrid, you wouldn't want it in your mouth, good or evil, makes you sick....'

'I fear you're stuck in time, in myth,' I say: 'Beside the big boss, firm in her chair, there sits death, and on the other side, salvation – both with liar dice in their hands, each has a multitude of arms – in each others' pockets, up skirts, in pants, their own, their neighbours'. You can make deals with them, but you won't honour them, and nor will they ... they give you the itch, the pox, they turn your liver into pepper soup, your brain....'

'A big prawn cracker,' she says.

'Listen,' I say, 'Tell me when you plan to leave, I'll help make the noise, the silence, that you need to cover your adventure ... retreat, desertion, the victory, anabasis ... But then – I'll drop away. I'm a deserter, it's my nature....'

'Betrayer,' she says: 'A plant. A spy.'

'I don't fit in your clan,' I say, 'Your tribe. I don't want to be like you, be sympathetic to what you want, and if it's nothing that you want to be, I don't want that. You hunt me. You're my bad choice, my twisted destiny, my scut that I can't hide when I hide from you; my giveaway. I have to leave, escape, and to escape from you but you're the only ones who leave, escape, so I must escape *with* you ... and turn you in to the justice you believe in, you defy, and that there's not.'

'Exactly so,' she says: 'You're one of us that we must extirpate. You're sick, diseased, pitiful and you will die ... we hope it will be quick and on your own, without consolation, without a cure – and yet we think your death will come too late. You spread it, you're the carrier, and because of you we all shall die, you bring the plague, you bring the universal – death....'

A crowd has gathered round us two, our joust, she the philosopher with flaming hair and megaphone. I remember Solomon, Solomon Crow, his farewell – 'You would not tell my story, tell and give me life,' he said: 'My life, told by you, is yours....'

'No, no,' I said, 'I can't do that. Take over others' lives and lose my own. It's your invention, I'm not part of it, your story, your confession – your walk to the guillotine – that's up to you. I'm not accomplice, not to that ... It isn't you, for sure, it isn't me ... no, it can't, it mustn't, be.'

'But complicit to much else, you are,' she says: 'Everybody is; complicit to terrible deeds they haven't even heard of....'

'The tribute they exact,' I press on, 'It's not forced. There's attraction, and people leave for where there's Something; or so it seems to them.

'I like to see you discuss and travail, you want none of the old façade which anyway – is no more. But I know you – you'll look for destiny, for something pungent, hot chillies, flags, peyote ... You'll look for people your executioners can practise on, you'll settle into gangs that share the power....

'You've seen that style is all you have, and that it's empty, vapid. Noise and silence – you have cancelled time and history, you've cancelled action, meaningful acts and significant intent. It's magnificent, a great invention – but,' and I start to shout, to scream, 'That will not get us out of here, or out of Somewhere! *Everywhere* is Somewhere, the ubiquitous. You are a blank, a pause, a rest. And still *it all goes on!*'

We walk, we argue. The water – 'if only it was drinkable,' she says: 'Making the noise – it's thirsty work.'

'Empty rafts,' she says, 'Lots come down. They're bad luck. And we can't climb in with anyone, and we don't know where we'll end ... or start.'

'I'm an important guy,' I say: 'I have survived. That means great forces were against me. If there's an escape, I know where we'd go. Down to the sea. That's not a destination, I know: and it's best you keep quiet, as we drift ... We, you and me, we risk losing our identities when we flee. I know it's what we want – and yet, and yet – when we are free to be our real, true selves – someone else will take the old ones, cast-offs – will that be enjoyable? Will it bear fruit?....'

Lili seems indifferent, if I stay or go. Is she planning ceremonies, different for each decision? A prize for good attendance, a 'godspeed' for when you go? I doubt it – here, ceremonies are banned – they're seen as substitutes for belief: – symbolic meets for party-loving sceptics. The idea is – 'believe, and keep it quiet', or 'be sceptical, let your doubts hang out, don't talk about them if somebody is interested....'

Here comes a big raft – overfull of elephants decomposing, melting – starting as six or seven individuals, now becoming one – a fearsome corpse: a dozen tusks, trunks pointed out like trombones, corroding, waiting for the downbeat.... huge parcels of grey skin becoming parched and lightened, like stinky cabbage rolls ...

'Clear them off,' I say, 'Make it our scene, there's room for all....'

There is no move. There's weakness, no resolve.

'There'll be no easier way,' I say: 'If you don't take your chance, the Noisy Crew is rubbish, a joke. Style? – perhaps. Posturing? A certainty.'

I repeat that to Lili: 'Is it good or bad?' I ask. 'The Noisy Crew – they let things out. The bad air we have inside, all of us – scream and shout. See if it works. Contradict. You do not live in truth, nobody does: – so, just say the contrary, you won't be further from what is true, you might be closer....'

'That's old stuff,' she says: 'Good, bad, true false – generations went mad answering those – it's an obsession, and look where we have landed? Is this good? Bad? True?'

'Those elephants,' I say: 'They're not native here, the river – usually it's a stream, a trickle – now there's abundance, and the animals are dead ... There was a cause – for them being, and for them being dead and putrefied....'

'You bury what is dead,' she says, 'Like you've buried almost everything – not in the ground, but inside you. There's an excuse for that – for all of us. The past is dead, not true, nor false – all of us, we're full of it. Good and bad don't count....'

'Is that what you say, tell your friends?' I ask, exasperated: 'Of course the past – it isn't good or bad, but that's not where the argument lies. Bad things are done, you need to know the detail ... the past, the present, full of bad....'

'Yes, yes,' she says: 'We go through that, we talk about it and it doesn't change a thing. The good thing is to live apart – live where bad is controlled as far as possible, comes from outside....'

'From us?' I ask: 'From people exactly like you, the same?'

'Who else?' she asks: 'That's where the puzzle starts. That's maybe why you want to get away – to where most people do not care. Don't know how to make the arguments.

'No children, no continuity, no place for the dead – it's an odd life, I know, living logically, avoiding the worst by living in it ... It's temporary, like everything, but – odd's the word. Here, there's no room for indifference, and none at all for people storming in, full of need and plans – a danger, novelties you can't control, people ... who ... People who ...' She pauses, talked out....

'Don't I agree with you?' I say: 'I know that's the paradox: escaping means going where – quite probably – conclusions about the bad, the past, are not at all what you would want. Quite the contrary of what you had arrived at. Yet – the motivation – it remains ... Life so tough, so bad, escape's imperative.'

'What would you want?' she asks: 'As a test? A war? Here? Good and bad?'

'"Here" doesn't enter in,' I say: 'Unless you want me to stay here, with you....'

'No, no,' she says: 'I'm quite indifferent. You don't come into anything important – not important to anyone at all.'

That's true. That's why I want to get away – from the indifference here, from mine and theirs. And that is why the Noisy Crew attracts – you can't be indifferent to them – the noise intolerable; the silence you are called to fill.

'Empires,' I say: 'They're the biggest things we can imagine. They float in front of us, like those rotting elephants. They bring stability, destruction, and war and peace: *Voina i mir.*'

'Crime, and punishment,' she says: 'Now, punishment is usually crime. State terror, disasters – natural and probably ... not. Crime is a punishment, and criminals are punished, and if they aren't – that is a punishment for everyone.'

'I used to play this game,' I say, 'Of opposites who turn out to be twins; or oneself in the mirror looking out ... when I was small.

'I'm still quite small ...' We laugh.

Down by the river, that's where I feel myself, my element. The rafts go by, sometimes there's an eddy, rapids, and they waltz, twirl round, dip and lift – sometimes there's dead, sometimes there are moribunds – disease or hunger – nothing to be done –

sometimes the people have weapons, and they shoot at us, throw spears or clubs, or whirling sticks that home back to their hands.

I say, 'We could fight back. One day they'll hurt someone, someone of us.'

The lady, my first, my only, Noisy interlocutor asks, 'Why? What good would it do? And are you one of them? knowing about rafts, what's on them, the danger? Maybe you came here on one, even one you made yourself ... wanting a better life and uninvited.'

'Yes,' I say: 'Sneaking in. We all have been, all who wait here to escape – we all fought to get on the raft, stay on, push the surplus off, destroy the marauders.... Yes, of course, I know it all, exactly what to do, have done it, lots of it; not everything, of course, enough to make my way, survive, when situations were impossible, and I could be exploited, where people I was close to turned out to be indifferent to me, a danger even.... Kill or be killed. Find someone to do it for you if you can't. Look away. Run if it gets too close.'

'You killed?' she asks.

'I was always on the other side,' I say: 'Afraid that they would kill me. *Certain* of it. Or, worse – ignore me. Pass me over, not here or there, useless, a nuisance, a disobedient slave ... barrack-room lawyer... Human rights and decency? ... chiliasm, rebellion, uppity, knowing too much ... The threat eternal. Just talk, from me; and if it led to action by another, well, that's bad luck, even good, who knows: who does the sums?'

'Always one or other,' she says: 'You're bold, take risks, cross the line, and then you're targeted. You too. Poor thing,' and she hugs me, just like Lili did, until it gets too much.

*

At night, the river bank – the eyes, the tails, light up. The hunt is on, for sex and food. A time of carelessness, of urgency: – watch it! those owls! Flash too bright – you're done, you're down. Part of the pellet, feathers and bones.

In the dark, in my black space by the surging river, black water full of invisible plashy birds – I need a raft, small enough that I can't offer space to Lili, the Searcher: nor the Noisy Huguette, or Hugo as she wanted to be called, if calling could be heard ... through the noise-makers or the silence ... Hugo Ball, her Dada hero. Namesake ...

My craft ... No dogs on board, no children, and you could add – no sex, no disagreements, no strong drink, no drugs – since we all are wearing clothes of fortune, without pockets, and indeed without coin – there being no acknowledged state, and no exchange –the only use is for ourselves. Our pleasure, and our fun?

'What for?' I asked: 'No coin; no sale or buy....'

'Your clothes must carry you, and you alone,' they said.

'Ah!' An answer to another question – slides in. 'No production? No needs, no exploitation?'

'Relax. Just clothes.'

A raft? And will this do? It could be a side from off a packing-case. I climb aboard. First stop – the Fairground – I was told it was an obstacle, and then there'd be the next, the shaking and the roar, quick-sands and whirlpools, the flaming flaring stove-pipes, playing their organ symphony of soot and lava.

The Fairground – it's obligatory. Joy, risk and cure – no longer try your strength, your aim, or even testosterone ... and off you go, but every booth, ride, you take, you are examined, tested, your nerves, your sniping ... the pennies rolled, horses, cocks mounted, raced, and never a winner on the roundabout. In frozen file, your chances fixed and framed, then home, if home you have, yourself tried through and through, departing with the hard-won sugar clouds and plushy toys. Examined – your body, soul, transferred and filed – objective records, never cancelled, nor revealed.

Here – the tests are serious. After the 'tunnel' – ghosts or love – there is a tent, a check-up for the itch, for putrefaction.

After the big dipper ride – shaken and scared, off you must go, to trauma centre and the ECG ... The osteopath when you have tried your strength, the oculist when you have shot your ducks ... Your fortune? Will it be better or dodgier once it's told? Your fortune is your health; that tells your future, puts it into months or days ... Life measured, minutes and years ascribed. No guarantee.

Your destiny? Is the magician interested in us, in anyone? Is it a scam, or arbitrary ... The tarot – a tarradiddle ...? This fairground, its exclusive side-shows – it explores in depth; your insides outed; no verdict from the shifty lady with the cloudy ball – rather, a print-out with your life expectation....

How long, how long? Life. This is it? Try to avoid the gloomy fair – they put a boom across the river so you must go in ... the tests, the vaccines, prohibitions, hums and ha's – the probe, the latexed finger up and up ... the sample, under the lights that see right through you, the tractions – cough up, spit out and quiz the gob! A picture of your liver? – perfection from the hidden silent dark, no palette could aspire to such a truth in black and white ... those pumps and filters, working while you sleep, or fall in love, or speak with tongues until ... they choke: they stop.

The three old ladies, as you leave – one knits, one tats, one crochets – take your pressure, pinch your bum, listen to your tell-tale heart ... You're certified – 'alive: discharge', everyone the same. 'All the fun of the fair, and don't despair ...' a fortune cookie – all the same....

So, there are people, a multitude, lined up and hopeful – immortality the prize ... lots and lots of piddling gimcrack wins; warnings and reprieves, and yet – each knows the future, theirs and everyone's, and why the present weighs, the breath grows short, limbs droop and disobey, the brain plays at Tom Tiddler's ground, finding false gold, then grannie's footsteps, one step forward, several back ... and yet, and yet ... hope, faith?....

Nothing is revealed, no life eternal, no resurrection, no certainty or stability; there's miracles a-plenty, but you're stuck, shut in your body and your ignorance ... Luck and ancestors prevail, determine....

Tomorrow? Perhaps ... Good health will keep you vertical until you die, the bullet hits, the blast turns bones to sticks of chalk....

Good while it lasted, maybe not so good ... The body and its soft centres unpredictable and shaky ... the memories, they come and nest and leave their fluff like eider ducks and then ... they're gone. Hello, goodbye ... maybe another year will bring an egg? ... Time now to leave those ducky chicks, that look exactly like you do....

The bill. Here it is, the bill for having nothing, no defects, being alive, a bill immense – it's clear, that if you're dead, you cannot pay, although ... your family tree? You are the living fruit, the knowledge and the ill, the well ... You pay for their ill-health, the ancestors: their prejudices, their wars, their depredations, slaving, ignorance ... or pass the parcel, the wriggly genes – pass them to your kids....

*

It's clear. There's organisation. Is there a plan? I didn't wait to see the circus – that round tent's the universe, and I've seen it all before – the clowns, the de-natured animals walking on two legs, trapezers, the funambulists – the flying ladies ... those who fly, who risk, who balance ... they have the net, the one that gathers you and saves you ... Omnipotent, the Ring-master, who directs the show, although we didn't vote for him: ... Wagner on sawdust, with tarararaboomdeay ... the organisation is extreme, but then, it finishes. It's done.

When the artists feel restored – another show, exactly similar. That finishes too, but there is no end, no conclusion. Round, and round. Horses, or elephants.

*

Organisation, everyone in place; the rebels too, the conformists and the neutrals. But – no plan. There is no end to anything – although a kind of end will come when we are compost ... the end of history, of human ingenuity, of capitalism, of socialism – all finished, false projections, lantern shows, maybe a celebration, a faith, a gadget, manuscript, a gala night, memorial, but ... there is no plan. Who'd make the plan? No, like the ants, the storks – like everything; there is an organisation, but no plan.

Look out! There's rapids, and I spin and tilt ... no plan. Don't look for it – you're in the organisation, or excluded, and opposed, and there's an end to it, sort of – except, the organisation organises everything – dissent and waste and sabotage as well, builds its defence, its walls – and WHOA! I'm in the river, being carried down, over the rocks ... what chaos! the noise, the fire above, the shaking, they're enlarged, I'm right upon them, unarmed, defenceless – rocks below and on the surface – empty rafts, sharp edges, heavy slabs ... the whirling arms and dragging legs....

In tranquil times – cells, plankton, are the origin of everything – life, air, variety – us and our brother, sister; cod and ostriches. It's all organised. There must have lived, been, the universal common ancestor. Everything's explained. The dialectics of nature? It seems a nonsense – only humans experience, acknowledge, dialectics – if anybody really does. You submit, or else – complain. But if it's all in cells, the start, the cycle – all is dialectics, everything.

Or it's not. What your eyes tell you – it's avoidable; dance to the music, don't let it enter in. Time kills you, dialectics confuses you. History: that's the torrent, tears your head off, lets you babble on about the dialectics, false realities, the spurious irreconcilables. Matter transforming as it must, all organised, ends endless but no end? Irrelevance: you have the revelation, and it does no good at all. Look closely – it's a tombstone....

Humans are a trial and error shot, castles of cells, rampant plankton, re-cycling, differentiating, nothing to write home about, or write anything particular about at all. A prototype? Snide poems written on the sand?

A graphic novel? – all that is required to open every mystery – when really there are none, no mystery. Lying pictures. There's just cells. But –

Falling in the water, you don't think like that. You thrash around, oppose the cycle, death – not natural, not to be welcomed as you might – if you were a mayfly, or one of the abundant babies of a crocodile – a surplus, an ephemeral, a spare ... so, down you go, the mass lives on but – No! Going under – you are intimately you, yourself. Save the ego at whatever cost – struggle against a chaos, disorganisation, an offence to the plan you made to glorify yourself, of which you are the king and queen, the lynchpin, only begotten ... You.

I'm spun and twirled – and cast upon the shore.

*

'This must be the gardener,' I hear a voice. Oh no – will the speaker be a deity, a faith that I've traduced, belittled – even challenged? If figures so – especially as it's got things wrong. I'm not a gardener.

'Yes,' says another voice: 'Exactly as I said.'

'Nothing is exact, said or not,' I think, I try to say: 'There's dialectics. You have to watch – the curve ball ... and sod's law....' The words don't come, they can't be tongued.

'He's thin,' the first voice says, 'But wiry. Taller than us. The gut is full of water, and the heart has paused. Plug him in and start him up.'

And that they start to do, it seems.

I never expected much. I know nothing about gardening, except it's the easiest of all careers ... no one knows what works, a few know the names of local plants – but so what? No one knows why leaves turn red, how to make fresh soil, how to make a picture, a diet – infallible – from planting stuff ... so that it doesn't wither, grow exorbitant with heat, not so it can't bear fruit, or only crabby goitres, inedible and full of mites....

I know as much as anyone. Not much.

'We don't want to start over,' says my rescuer, and the friend – each had seized an arm to pull me up the bank and pump me out. 'We want a new beginning. Not a start that finishes as we did.

'No names, and no beliefs. No sexes. And no territories, no bosses, no crowns, no languages ... we all speak the same, make love as it seems best, address each other by whatever word or sound or gesture that attracts ... Each may believe, if having faith in things invisible they must – but keep it to themselves....'

'It sounds delightful,' I say: ' – but ... there will be gangs and poisoners, embezzlers and bullies, magicians and warrior chiefs – a beginning for sure becomes a starting over ... not repetition, necessarily, but something like. It's in our destiny, our matter, our tiny confined brains ... we shall invent, but all will transmogrify into power, to systems of oppression, classification – all that you want to improvise will freeze, solidify. We shall not tramp the world and settle where it's welcoming – we'll be corralled, instructed, socialised and schooled ... We shall need fixed characters and temperaments, like actors in a film, psychologies like in a story of two hundred years ago – the canons and the cannons will prevail, horror is normality, disaster the default.... We love the continuity – we needn't like the fixity, it's there whatever comes....'

'Well,' says my rescuer: 'Let's try. I'm sure I'm right – although I don't insist ... this is the way to begin, and end up in another place, different from what has led to our catastrophe....'

*

I cultivate my garden – so that we can eat. It doesn't go too well, no lustre, it's not philosophy. But there it is.

People? The nameless ones, faithless and experimental, we – they – are growing like freak novelties in our shells – hatching as a fresh congeries of dinosaurs, vegetarian, some fletched so that they might – in emergency – take wing. It's wonderful. It's home at last, free, everywhere and everyone is ours, is us, our imaginations bear us to the heights and depths, each has a sufficiency, invents themself in-finitely....

It's not for me. It's contentment before a fall. I don't believe in it ... I need not, but I don't. I leave them when the harvest's due, the flowers, the little birds, the moths, the butterflies, the bats ... I'm emptied out, eyes open: the sky! The greatest nothingness. The trees, so green when up I bubbled, up from the green bottle I was corked in, burst out of in a blast of ... Where's everything?

The trees, they are no more ... The garden – enough of it!

I wonder how it all turns out.

I take the raft again, it's stuck in the mud, where I washed up ... escaping death, escaping people, illusions: – what next can I escape?

*

'The sea, the sea' – I'm not enthusiastic. There's survivors on our makeshift rafts, all round. The flaming stovepipes, and the swarms of 'quakes – those are ahead. There is a pulse, a beat....

'What's happening?' I shout: 'Must we turn back – I have no appetite for that....'

Someone shouts back – 'The tide, the tide – it runs against us, whichever way we turn. Are you a survivor? If you are, remember – someone's always left to testify, or if there's no one, take your pen, your chisel – or find a stylus that will make a sign on bark –

birch, for preference, since the taiga runs on uselessly, on, into infinity, a universe of trees inedible – and write the epic, our last stand....'

'Who are they, our opponents?' I shout back.

'Who's done wrong, and who revolts? We all have grievances – don't state yours, you'll end up dispossessed and on a list. Just aim at passing through the lines ... the flames will dry the ground: the machines that shake and skim what's left – they'll turn up treasure, that's the scheme – jewels for us all, perhaps ...' the voice shouts out.

'But I'm unarmed,' I say: 'And cowardly.'

'If you see a soldier, friend,' the voice comes back, 'Just point your finger and say 'bang'. Maybe he or she will do the same – at least she'll know who you are, and what's the threat exactly that you pose....'

'No, no,' I say, 'Exact knowledge – there is none....'

We press ahead – the massacres proceed.

'The end is peace,' the disembodied voice proclaims, 'It always is.'

I hear the voice again – the prophecy: 'This is not apocalyptic fantasy, that weary genre. It's what has happened from the start, will go on happening – till there's an end or an infinity, and remember: you won't see either one....'

'I'll get through,' I say, 'Through to the other side, and then again, if it must be ... back, over and over....'

Who am I speaking to, I ask myself....

'Your foot!' says the voice – mellow and fruity: maybe a mezzo stooping down below the stave, a baritone, lightening up?

I look down – it's a claw, a bird's claw, as if they'd bound my foot, to show I'm not a menial, but a fancy lady. On land, I'd hobble; in the sea, who cares?

'You'll fall,' the voice says.

'No, no,' I say: 'If there were trees, I'd perch. The foot is charred, it's true. Too bad.

'I'll soldier on, the same struggle: – over and over.'

I sing – 'win my partner, loot the crown, invent the rhyme, hammer the sonnet into shape ... milk the cow, and pick the fruit – and tap tap tappity-tap-tap-tap – like the smith, I'll tinker round the golden claws that clasp the jewel'....'

And a crowd joins in, singing as if it was a roundelay, and us the artisans of strife, successful and victorious ... like a panto, maybe like Offenbach; or an Internationale of dare and plod....

It's rousing stuff, bad cess to who might say it's not – alas, it doesn't straighten out the foot, but nonetheless it warms the blood and sutures up the heart....

It's not a plan, a mission – those have been replaced, by an indifference to anything except 'survive'. Some fight for that, the world preserved: and others want to see it burn and flood. It's medieval, back five hundred years ... The power? We're impotent. And liberation? It's lost its pull.

When you get too smart and beaten down – it's true, the struggle nought avails. Is that it, is that all?

The drying ground's been broken up – small tarmac slabs, as if they're hinged, folding like board games – Monopoly, perhaps. Even if they're broken small as small – they are not soil, nothing will grow. There's shaking – as if the whole will fall into a huge hole, or maybe something will be born, earth-hued, a mulch of all humankind so far, fertile with inventive cells – a million years compressed into a dragon-shape, all scales and swish – not starting over, nor yet something new. It's what we can expect, on this miscalled 'earth', the only one with human figures clinging on, existing in a universe without an end, without creator ... Perpetual evolution. Change, reacting to chance, quick slow chance: change. Something seeming to emerge, and then you see it's variations, with a theme of stalks; growing, writhing upwards, throwing out huge pods of beans that will make you fart like molten thunder – then, dying, falling back as harmless halms.

Shallows, a shallow lake, low shores – a sea loch.

'Hey!' I call out to a fellow paddler – unisex and stooped, poling, and chattering with fear and concentration: jabbering some syllables, 'Hey! Listen to this, what I just thought up!'

'I heard:' the guy replies – the voice, plummy for a man, orotund for a woman: 'You're a born *jongleur,* a *chansonnier.* Seeking the crowds, their acclamation – but always on the move, a down-and-out, some crook's crooked yes-man, seditious jester....'

'No,' I say: 'I conclude. I am my context, my only comrade and companion. Performing isn't it at all, it's not my thing ... not "being another thing"....'

'Of course it is,' the navigator says: 'It's just the audience is you and you alone. Most of us is like that ...

'Novelty – time brings it every hour – it drives us on, revives or stuns. See – a new front opens – we advance with style. Style. Is all there is....'

And that is true. We've nothing else, and I must punt along, and bear with my painful scorched and blackened leg, even as the poling finds a new consistency beneath the sticky water – sand, gravel, stone ... a bottom; the punting's heavier, easier to keep a line, but, exhausting:– 'we could stop here, build a castle or a wall.... and yet ... Who's attacking, who's to defend? Are we the barbarians or are they – and does it matter anyway?'

And since there is no 'they': just 'us'?

'What is the mark of being human?' asks my fellow paddler: 'Apart, of course, from being its only example in the vastness of this universe?'

'I know!' I shout: 'Symbolic representation. That is the distinguishing accomplishment.'

Each time a different answer. Is someone grading them?

*

There's calm. We, we who've been paddling towards the sun, we make an island of all the makeshift rafts – some tiny, some enormous with soggy divans and chairs made out of other chairs, men bearded, women covered up – kids swaddled ...

The lucky – with retainers, gangs – they shall be boss!

We are lots, exultant, torn through by voyaging. There'll be much to fight for – between ourselves: and whoever we just beat, or are escaping from. My leg should drag me down, and save me – from people who might challenge me, my poor thoughts, all the years spent on the waves, scavenging, leeching on to people poorer even than I was ...

What will the fight give us? 'The revolutionary imperative of spilling blood' – yes, I believed that, then I did not. Absolutely. Now – I'm on the fence. Count me in and out – it will all happen anyway, the violence. Don't bother asking, and don't justify.

As they say, 'Soldiers surrendering? Shoot them, somebody!'

Pirate captains and beggars have lost a leg: mine trails, but is not lost – it may help me, as an entertainer. Harder to throw me out the bar – a dead weight, winning sympathy....

We peer around, like ghosts just waking up. And are there other ghosts, the lemurs? What's happened? Where did the ghost, the lemurs, go? Nothing, nothing that we did, and so – just destiny, kismet. No fault, the guilty ones – all dead.

Songs? A philosophy? Stoicism – this time it's me the slave. Before, the philosopher contemplated slaves, his slaves, and he advised – 'Take what comes, put up with it.' That – for him – was good philosophy. Not so good for slaves.

The guy with the wet furniture tells me 'You need an agent. I don't engage the artist – artists are intrusive, pester. I don't want to hear your sad song – they're all the same, all good. I've plans

– for entertainment, art, but for that you need first to find some food and drink.'

What's happened? So, am I a courtier in a new regime? A dream, hallucination? Why not.

The campaigns, protests, my life as frontline soldier, burnt in my trench, shipwrecked – a sequence of catastrophes ... Can I forget all that and find an agent? Someone who'll sell me?

'Many of the best minstrels have been lost,' says the impresario: 'It'll take months to replace the songs. You'll do your best, I hope.'

*

It's awful, being rare. Like the sloth, the ant-eater, the blue frog ... there's only millions of me left. Will I be conserved? Like on a reservation, special, apart, unequal. Not a barbarian, but an onlooker, an outlooker; feathered but not a bird ...

The history – it made sense at the time, living it, but not now. When I invent myself, or rather, the reasons for being me, I'll invent a meaning for the history ... All around, just aimless matter, mulching down and waiting, maybe to become something quite splendid, like ospreys, but till then ... shades.

As dry land emerges, the boss is giving names, dividing up resources. Countries? Create rich little places; big ones – immense but poor ... I feel it's a mistake, but then, the club is his; the scribes, the sculptors – and the minstrels: we come from the waves and set up as we can.

He runs the show, him and his mates – imagination, execution – they're all his.

'People? In line, waiting, expecting?

'Keep them coming in....'

Light and joy. Being what I want, and more. What other people want, all soaring, up together.

Surely, not too much to hope....

*

We're still on rafts – some have a roof, my boss has found some surly dogs who prowl around. Up high the birds are back – big, and black. Could they be condors? Like the albatross, they never land, nor sleep – they cruise and doze, they have no song.... a flourish? Call-sign?... nothing you could hear on earth.

'And you've no voice,' my boss tells me: 'It's awful – like a horse.

'I'll put you in my entourage – not to entertain, nor fool around.

'My people must be celibate – for you, it's a relief. You're not cut out for a relationship ... too much of niggle-niggle – thoughts and questions ... quite exhausting.'

'Well,' I say: 'Your judgement's yours and yours alone, but then – I need a job, or rather, cash, to help me get away.... But tell me now, what is the work, and don't conceal the difficulties....'

And that he does.

'It's very simple, learnt in a flash,' he says, ' – you do exactly what I tell you to.'

1

SHARDS

I used to collect old coins. Very old coins. I discovered places and dead people, vainglories, I bet you've never heard of.

'SONIA'S THERAPY'

Across the desk – she wears ... all I can see: a turtleneck. It hides her sag – the jowls, the throat. Turtle. What a misnomer: the armoured turtle evoked to name the shapeless wool, the empty skin. Whoever thinks up what we need as common knowledge, words to keep us marching, sometimes in step, on and on – they don't know anything ... no eyes, no fancy: no respect.

'What do you mean? Signify?' Sonia asks: 'Where are you, along the road? Or are you jumping off the roof? Don't you wish there was a session where you could say exactly where you are, what you've discovered? ...? No? So, what are you?'

The envelope beneath her hand says: 'Test.'

*

'You make jottings,' she continues. 'Important – but just ignore the questions, and your answers too. I'm here to make you better, not quiz you. Think of me as – a curer. My body, my status – remember? Below, a saint: above, a doctor.

'I ask you – 'what do you want to say?' Then, we have to test what you mean, not what you say. There's no punishment, it's not that kind of test. The test is the test of the test, not of you. I believe the test works; runs on from subject to subject – straightens out your skeleton. As you age, you collapse into yourself, get smaller, and distort. Bone crunches into bone, pinches the muscles and the nerves: – the brain – my! How it runs on, even when your instructions aren't obeyed. The system's choked and blocked....

'The random, the crazy – it's become their time ... Are you senile? We know you are, your age tells everything. Hurry, hurry, with the answers – if you're dead, there are none. How does your mind work? How does anyone's? Reality: do you separate it from all that's not real ...? How? Is that the same for everyone? How do we know – we know you lie, all of you. Why find if you're senile, what you did before senility – we might have to imprison you, execute you, or many others instead of you ... A can of worms, that's what your brain looks like.

'Climb on this low bed. I know it hurts. Lying down? – you've forgotten how. You fear you might fall off, go straight down, the floor won't stop you, nor the earth.

'It's real, the pain – everything is real, just like you say. We all live in the real: we know we do. We think we do: – cross fingers!

'Stretch out. The pain takes over – you're agèd, pain is all that matters – hoping to end the pain without also being dead. An impasse. But there's the past! Try stepping back into it, avail yourself of it: – it's languages that no longer have a speaker. It's art. Original.

'The wheel was spun for you – you lost, like everybody. You got old age, and disappointment. You're reactionary.

'I'll sort you out. You're right to summon me.'

*

Not many people seem to have an interest in you, your body, and your quirks. Whoever does – instantly becomes a friend, as well as therapist.

Here I am, on the bed – a special bed, denying sex and sleep. I think of writing about it all. That's my defence, my 'second thoughts'. Does it work? I doubt it.

WRITING SOMETHING DOWN

My notebook:

What do we mean by 'every abstraction'? Isn't there just one abstraction – like 'every height': things must have one, a height. Things have abstractions – so, do abstractions have things? Am I right – abstract and abstraction: – the same? Who to ask?

Does every abstract-abstraction produce an incarnation, a solid ghost, and can those be sloughed off, to die; those realities incarnate? – observe their diaphanous skins, the prancing devils! Look in the pit – those corpses don't exist? Only as their ghosts? Are they abstractions? Oh no! Or – oh, yes, that too!

And yet.... we stalk the abstraction, the abstract, flag the journey to those who plod after us, and then we come to see that everything we see is nullity, the incarnations, the journey, the demons, all intercourse: – no Other, and no Others. All we want – is the meaning, the hope, of abstractions. We clutch at butterflies, the abstractions in which we strive to live and understand: – to catch?

We surmise that we're on a journey where each stage has a post-inn, pre-mapped, on post-cards.... a travel, travail, which negates itself – a post-modernity, post-realism. A piece of track which can't be revisited, re-traversed. Everything is something, and is nothing, abstract and concrete. Is something and becomes nothing. Nothing and something. Fleeting and real, the concrete: or empty and permanent, the abstract.

Every panorama is also the fog that obscures it. Hear the post-horn sounding through the gloom....

Abstract – a special kind of nothing. Concrete? Slick as a frozen pond. Watch it as it melts.

The flesh beguiles, deceives ... Try it – it's a dare, a short-cut. Find a partner – look into your partner's eyes unceasing.

But – don't be taken in by slippery reality. It's here today, quite different tomorrow. Exalts you, casts you down – indifferent, malicious.

Socialism – there's an abstract. I gave – it took – my life.

SELF-ABSORPTION

I think: – I have always been a genius. Like 'always a pheasant' if you are one. Not like 'always a hero': – you couldn't last.

Some people are malign, unpleasant. 'Your opinion', of course, but it's to you it matters. How do you deal with them? You find often one such is married to you, sleeps beside you, commands you if you are a soldier, bosses you anyway if you are not. Your best friend stealing things you value – money too ... how do you react? Maybe it's the nature of relationships, that all, or almost all, are with unpleasant people, and maybe to them *you* are one of those, the horde of malignant individuals – who send them to war, corrupt their values, torment, insult them ... give them a medal.

Truth? Art, invention ...? Here's a start –

'You're not honest with me,' he says: 'Your relative's due, you didn't say.'

'You don't respect women,' she says. 'Why should I be straight with you?'

'The station-master said the sleigh was ordered, to meet the morning train.'

'My brother will take me back with him,' she says: 'To the great city: he won't meet with you.'

She leaves at once, but I have him living in the house with me, until the soldiers come and burn it down.'

It needs background, something not trivial.... We're in the mist: the wars, the droughts, the floods.

Every idea – a universal lesson, if you're in school that day. Next day – another diatribe, a new emergency.

Where are the lessons of the day before? Socialism? 'If you're quite with it, it'll kill you, to show it's real.' 'They'll conscript you to fight it, and if you don't destroy it, it'll have you die, die in a ditch....' 'It's your life, your hope – what would you do without it?'

What won the patriotic war?

Sacrifice.

Socialism? Why the fuss? 'It's just another way of doing economics....' It used to be a big hope. Now – not a hope, not a threat, and there are no more promises.

It became like Buddhism: – the destination is consciousness: a journey to itself.

In 1970 – the motor stalled. Science was running away from it, the USSR. It couldn't keep up with the technology. A limit had been reached – never superseded; never since. Even the words became no longer current; 'Soviet'. 'Union'. 'Fusion'.

Everything new happened, goes on. No longer new. Old new, new past.

It's all past, all changed, the players and the text. Forgotten, erased – all the fuss, the forbidden dream faded, soured: that all could change, we'd make it change. Only the fear, the hostility, remains. Hostility – to what? To everything? Other people? What's left is an indifference to each of the many pretexts to end the world ... Or fear. Suspicion?

Carrying that long rifle with you all that time – its length should make it super-accurate ... At night it lies beside you, tall, getting taller. Keep it loaded? Don't exaggerate! Prudence. But, your unexpected erection sneaks inside the trigger-guard and – "Fire! Bang! Off with your head!"

*

All gone by, all ridden out and exhausted, like the diligence, the black horses.

To make a spiritual journey, a pilgrimage, touching the bright spots – you need a body. Can you manage it, if that's all you have, a body?

Trivial, alas. I haven't hit a target. Haven't aimed off for wind, the wind that wafts the concrete.

NEGATIVE ASSESSMENT

The test continues. She looks over what I've written, deflates it, and me.

'Hmmm,' she says: 'Bits. Not even pieces. You're not at home in this stuff. The mystic tongue – won't wag for you. The ordinary people – they don't live and talk like that. Catastrophe bursts in, it hasn't been discussed and parsed, analysed, not like you believe. Besides – it's gone, wheeee! Another calamity bounds in, off and away; and disappears. There's always other things to fear, mustered ready to assault you, to bear you off.

'You forgot your relatives – they were Russians, long ago, but all they remember now is civil war. How it lasted, lasts, will last forever. And see how staid and stodgy they all are; *pirozhki*. Enemies of civilisation? Of yours, maybe? Try to be serious! You, I know – you have no country.

You've something else? What? A joust with time, with probabilities?

'We were lovers, if you recall. Now, I'm here to straighten you out – no rancour, and no secrets. You've lost the atlas, and the compass.

'More supplies! Pills! Smoke! Beer! You need another six-pack of commonplace to help you step out again ... proud as a Mughal prince!'

*

I write down – 'I'm interested in limits. Limits of our powers and intentions – of the species, and then of the earth – it's not a stable object, not even round ... a curate's egg, indeed – sometimes temperate and fruitful, more often rough and raging red.

'Then – I'm intrigued by consequences. How to plot a line between something and the something quite different it's produced, as it goes percolating through time. Some things, we say, are foreseeable, others not only unpredictable, but – metamorphoses.

'That's it! Metamorphoses. What are the limits to a something that changes into another thing? The butterfly – who'd have guessed? The infant – its silent set of unused bones, waiting for the undertaker. Origins incredible!

'Consequences, causes, effects. What inventions! As if creation could make links, a chain – when everything flies apart in our imagination. Games – to find the logic, order – one thing following another ... "thing"?

'No – we are Creation now. Creation was once the wind. Everything that is. The huge wind, the universe, that's there for nothing save itself, making space, time: – unfathomable, incalculable. Certainly "unliveable" and "inconceivable". Now, we're the only Creators – the rest was done – "for us", "to us". We Create: eddies, swirls, marsh-gas. We bodge.

'We've done badly, now we want to ride the windy void – and that's a big mistake.

'Think of the starlings, who can make a pattern on the wind. We can't. It means? Nothing. It's "what we are is what we do". Starlings: – Stalins, my mother thought the word must be.

'If we could paint what *we* are – what a horror! I suppose we have – with help – painted the world; a dun colour, linked by canals of slime, discharge – and tiny tin ships, up and down.'

'I thought you were interested in abstraction,' she says, briskly: 'In reaching the highest state of consciousness – the inside; or "yourself". And not yourself. Being, truth, enlightenment. The outside, in short. Both.'

I know this is a trick – she wants to take me where I don't want: another inexistent place, that makes me feel like someone else. I say –

'You're wrong: I don't think it's fruitful, all that stuff. A self-delusion, a rhetoric of nothingness.'

I'm old, but I feel concrete. In a week, a day, an hour – I die. 'I become an abstract ...' It isn't so, I know. But that's how it feels. I'm fascinated, terrified. Oh, to be both, abstract and concrete, for always ... or settle for the concrete, forget the abstract. Or the compromise? No, you can't! No immortality. But ... being abstract means being nothing, I'm convinced.

DON'T DESPAIR....

Sonia says –

'And yet – you made a start: a sketch for a story about "revolution", set in a Russia, somewhere.

'Then, a criticism, as you say, of exploration. Seeking some place, just off the map, but you've been told where it is – Nirvana, or at least a better reincarnation ... an "after-you", re-born with two legs, not four or six.

'All not original, and not revealing. A tough spot, where you've often been, and hope not to return.'

*

I want to speak, tell her – 'let's end it here, I'll pay in cash, forget the tax.'

Never tell an acquaintance you have a little problem – they know already, everybody does.

No notebook. No test. Start again, the slate is clean. 'Your peccadilloes – all forgiven – you didn't make good with any one of them....'

*

This is what I think...

They're the originals. Dogs. They adapt, grow bigger, and they'll come and get you all and eat your bones. Wolves – they know how to deal with space, and trot right through it. They don't have resentments, don't make vendetta.

You'll be surprised – you won't expect it, though you'll fear it: rage. It comes and hits you, scratches off your face. Only humans feel so angry, so much fury....

If you imprison people, kill them, steal their land, lord it over them, call them names and deride their history, their existence – they'll come for you! It happens, and the jailers – are always shocked, always surprised. Perhaps – it's what happened here.

Like in the nightmare – they'll come and throw you down the holes, all of you. Did you like them in the past, love them? – too late! Down you go, and if you run, there's machetes for you and all your clan, your ancients and the babies and sweet people befriended who seemed beautiful, and they'll decapitate your kids and rape you, it's orgiastic, unstoppable and not regretted unless you decide on vengeance in your turn ... but at the moment, it's pay-back fun, and justice, and right to be completed: to the last trace ... A dream – don't be surprised if it becomes real.

So much for meditation.

*

I know. I trashed a garden once. The gardener, my teacher – she'd oppressed me, systematically – I pulled up all her flowers and broke off the branches of the fruit-trees that promised much. The blossom, I remember its scent ... And they caught me, put me on show, and I didn't give a fuck, it was to be done, and I did it.

SHRIVEN AND BALD

I'm much younger now. I don't need to invent lives I've had. Battles won, observed, escaped. I don't answer questions from the test, don't then take refuge in the notebook.

'Live once, but live it full.' Print that on your shirt?

The cure-giver. Other people? – she doesn't understand. Can't follow a tight argument. She doesn't know that everything she is – her being free and true and just and empathic – excludes everything I, everybody else, can be ... our freedom must be independent of hers, quite incommunicable, indifferent to what she is. I'm free – it doesn't mean she is. We're independent, but not fixed within ourselves, our destinies. She could be free, but in her way ... free, and me her slave. Or turn about. Me – a slave, she free – she's never seen me, heard of me. I'm there, unfree. And lucky her: just, in her individual way, free.

My justice must stay far from hers, her justice can't be mine – the quality might be universal, but it's fragmented and particular, exists uniquely in, for, each one of us.

Think differently? – wow! Different from what? Reality? What a clash! What terror, and what terrorism. Think how reality could be changed, and go on, different. Just try it and you'll be in the shoot-out and then the prison ... forget those spacious German cells, with TV and the music stand – you're in a fetid space, the floor is carpeted with you, your lookalikes – if you could see them

... and you can't stand up, lie down, or walk around – you're meat in a small can.

Now! You know what being individual must mean . *You* know, and it doesn't matter, not a bit – the cell's too small except to hold too many guys, so many you can't see their face but what's of interest to you is *yours,* your face, it being different, invisible, unviewable, indifferent in that little space, and everybody with a face knows which is theirs and that it isn't yours.

Think differently? You'll bring it all down! We must all think the same, or it all melts.

'You don't understand?' I ask: 'Don't understand everything? If you understand anything, you understand it all, everything. No? You have no clue? It's all to do! Start – anywhere, at any age. Mostly, it's a slog, and even when and if you understand it all, everything – what does it do for you? All this is true, but it doesn't lead anywhere. That's a paradox. Truth should be valuable; knowing everything is not.

'As if...? As if we're free and equal, know who we all are? You must pretend, in fact. Shape-change, shuffle the cards, dethrone the kings – adopt more one-eyed jacks ... Surmise, suppose, hypothesise. It must be done that way. That's how the law gets written.'

She has no answer.

And yet: – 'as if'. It moves, all moves. The real's 'as if'. Turbulent and indecisive. It takes us anywhere, to anywhere at all.

THIRTY HORSES

It all changes. Light, bustle ... A noise you'll only ever hear the once in your life.

The big fire – there's thirty horses to be looked after. All terrified, all sick, wounded, bleeding, poisoned, suffocated. Hungry? Look after them – the herd, each individual. Each one is different, all have the same differences and you can't remember which one is which.

The smell: – smoke and shit. A choice meat dish. Wild.

Enough of therapy and questioning. Quick! Do something absolutely new!

She laughs: 'You're a horseman? One of the four? Who purify, destroy? I didn't suspect it....'

Hurry – don't answer back... She doesn't see, can't compose, the picture.

I have to save them all, each one. I hope no one rides any of them, never, not once, not one. And surviving should mean free, emancipation.

'Come on, this is urgent, this is something that must be done,' I say.

'I realise that,' she says: 'I'm not in it with you to have adventures. The fire, the horses – that's you, not me.'

'Knowing somebody's secrets doesn't make you an interesting person,' I say.

I tear a stale baguette into large pieces and stuff the flaking lumps in my pockets.

'There's nothing wrong with you,' she says: 'You're impenetrable. Some people are. Not everyone has to team up and couple in with other people – but it's a disadvantage being original if you want to communicate, or teach. Or be heard in any way at all.'

'When we were lovers,' I say, 'We communicated – I suppose. And now? What's the result? Who's learned what, who's been taught?'

She doesn't answer. I don't want answers, I'm still with questions. The horses – a herd of wild, or semi-wild – dark, all darkness. Loud with primal cries.

They jostle round, they paw at me – I see they're almost all in trouble – not mental? All kinds.

There is frenzy. They've profound burns, and maybe wounds from teeth and hooves ... they don't want bread, they want the much much more that I don't have.

A grass fire? Wildfire? Wild ire? Fireworks, or a rocket – a mistake, miscalculation, or just vandalism – a sabotage? Sprayed with gasoline: fear and rage.

Wild horses, like all animals, without a price, once an asset, now petitioners and fugitives.

A word comes to me – 'packing-needle'. That's what you need to sew them up with pack-thread, but wounds are multiplying – the horses are enraged, furious – they turn on one another, when a flank is throbbing, bleeding – they kick out at someone, some comrade, mother, brother – near to them, each afflicted with the same pseudo-anonymous authorship of their own, of everyone's, disaster. If there's no cause visible – then it's you! You bring it on yourself – *you* are creator, sole responsible – for what happens to you, where you end up, your trajectory. There's no external cause to see ... It's philosophy, touching on bearing, reversing, the stuff that happens – and they don't care about it – the 'how things are, could be': just to be changed, from savagery and pain, to convalescence. The cause, the remedy – mysteries: in you yourself.

Being care-free. We can't be. Not them, not me.

I should have brought a lantern, so I could see my full inadequacy ... there's little ones, foals, that seem unharmed, or maybe – they're the miraculous survivors every massacre requires.

If they decide to leave? To run off madly, furious, get away and find a sandy place, some water, far from humans: making a stockade, a rampart, of blistered bodies. Bodies stacked up against more unwanted evil ... defence, even when all attack has ceased, never attempted, probably.

'Help me, Sonia,' I shout. At least, to shape their minds.

'I don't know what to do,' she shouts: 'You were looking after them. Do something.'

Shoot them, shoot them all, and solve the puzzle, except we have no gun. No knife. No iron beam. No stomach. No way to cancel all the pain.

What would the movies tell? Shoot, shoot! Blanks.

I hate, reject completely, the procession of time, and all the furrow that it makes.

'Did someone hate them?' Sonia asks, with nothing better she can do: 'Not individually, but as a herd? Hurt them, have them face catastrophe, like we all say we do?'

Then, those that can – they're gone. Like wind on grass.

'They've gone to where you go where there's no help,' says Sonia.

'You were useless,' I say, 'You've no title to chart movement. To sprinkle reason.'

It's dark, you can't see hummocks – the grave, the corpse: the fall, the drop.

'They've gone where we shall go,' I think.

'They're going where we will,' Sonia says, and I scream at her: 'You, you who think only of yourself, your pleasures.... You are rooted exactly where I am, another failing scarecrow.'

It's what the Emperor told his sister, Marie Antoinette. That was 'consequences' – here, there's none. The horses run – into the future, into fate, destiny – oblivion. History.

Wild horses – corralled and fed, to help them out. To be sold?

'I just agreed to feed them,' I say: 'That was the deal – just a few days, until....'

'Responsibility – does it have a term, an area, a distance?' she asks: 'If I were you ... Being responsible – you need more than a good lawyer ... If I were you....'

'You are me,' I say: 'The animals know us – we're not them, but we are animals, like, and different, from them.

'You need to know what you experience. It's consequences, more than curiosity: – it's what you are and why you suffer, why we all do from just simplicity – the being here, living a life, no eternity, no judgement and yet – "it moves", always, it hurts. It should be, seem, static, but it swirls. We don't just eat and copulate and die, stand, sit – we suffer too.

'The way to understand the suffering is to start from evil. You, Sonia, the sufferer, me too. The end of the night – not dawn, but total darkness, the absolute. That way you understand – not the feeling, but where it starts. That dark door, unguarded, is where you pass to evil, it's obligatory if you would understand the horror... if there is evil, here it is. It starts here and you are always in it.

'I think, yes, a God would be merciful. He let the animals speak to one another, but not to us. We can't speak to them; nor they to us. It's a boon, a limit to our wisdom, thankfully.'

DESPAIR....

'I see you under stress,' she says: 'But what you are – I've no more idea than I had before. If it should happen many times – should I be any wiser? About you, about action? Process in general. Not panic – just impotence and bewilderment. You don't know what to do. You – like everyone?'

'It's about exploration,' I say, gaining time.

She says: 'Nothing in this story is about exploring. Exploring is finding a destination and suffering to reach it....'

'Exactly,' I say: 'But don't labour it.'

'Understanding suffering through knowing evil ... It sounds traditional. German. Enigmatic. Being evil? Or being in it? Close to ... Tempted ...' She wrinkles up her face, mouthing the last part of this.

'Oh,' I say: 'It's a clue, that's all. Clues are for you, not me, to follow. Maybe you won't get there. As for the horses....'

'Yes,' she says 'We know what will happen to them, every one, little and big, black and brown. With or without us. No evil ... much suffering.'

'They say ignorance is evil,' I say: 'They even say reducing ignorance reduces evil.'

'Now they're kidding,' she says, 'Maybe you avoided school, and didn't see?'

'They say suffering is evil,' I say, 'But they don't mean "is the same as". I don't know what they mean. "Engage with it", perhaps. It can't be that suffering is chance and evil's permanent – it could be the exact opposite....'

'Oh no,' she says: 'It's dangerous. Impossible. Keep off – it's not for you. And, once – you were baroque, elusive, overflowing: even rococo; an eel through times – a true Arcimboldo of connections, symmetries, anomalies that layered multitudes of worlds.... You were convinced, convincing – you could not be caught. You were the white fawn in the forest, then – you were the forest. You were both its protection and the soul in flight. You burst with life – life that lived on life; the tree, also its parasite. Now – you say you don't know what your formulation means. That is disaster. You ferried yourself to somewhere you don't understand.

'Once, you saw that all equations can refer to any Thing at all. It may be puzzle – but it's also clue and key. 'Why?' – go on, ask that!'

'You saw, Sonia,' I say: 'The horses. Discuss. Set your powers on them.'

And we leave it there.

*

All the shouting came much later, when the massacre was done. I was accused, acquitted because no punishment could fit my guilt. I – was the judge – who else? I, they, decided to shut everything within the mystery box – inside it's roomy, there's tiny evanescent gods and bone tallies of those who've disappeared without an explanation ... two tallies is enough, a giant's long bones, millions archived on them with little cuts.

All the horses died. They weren't notched on any tally.

LOVE, ETC.

The horses stood together – it got them nowhere. I tried – for myself, standing alone.

We are responsible for everything we do, don't do, and we are punished for what we haven't done by people we don't know ... by crows, men and women of the law, of the test, faces who don't speak our language.

Character and impulse – used to be attributed to culture ... the culture of blacks, of slaves, of dominant peoples, of everyone, maybe by extension on to horses, tigers, elephants. Elephants, yes, them for sure.

Where does culture come from? What does the species make of it, the cultures they say differentiate us, make lakes of us, shallow, deep, volcanic, draining, stagnant, dead and mostly – disappeared? Islands in the sea, lakes in the landscape – those were the cultures. Then came a culture, mother-of-us-all. One size universal – so, the differentiation lessened. We seem to come together once again. 'The species', as I say to Sonia: 'groping towards itself. Like before we split apart.'

Love? It's always brought in at this point.

Love? When it goes, it goes as completely as a kidney-stone. It's passed – if you catch it, calcified, a pebble – it's quite nondescript – a blob, a grey and black. You put it in the little box where you keep badges, paperclips and rings.

What does it mean, as Sonia asks: and what would that meaning signify? Do you need judges, divining spirits? Do they know: are they needed? Do they judge and recognise who you *really* are, think you are? Is there a plan for each? Drawn up by the evaluators, and never operable? If it doesn't rest on 'love', which is ephemeral, then let's say 'death', which certainly is not.

All have a culture: – who has love, has had love? Look in the tiny box.

FAREWELL TO THE USELESS

'The horses, Sonia,' I say.

'Nothing,' she says: 'They don't mean, not anything. Or else we just don't understand. It's our machinery: – it has no take, no travel. Mind is a jackhammer to stop up volcanoes....'

A pause....

'Snap out of this,' she says: 'Change country, landscape at the least, have an adventure. That's what you do. Trust me.'

'The house,' I say, 'It didn't burn.'

'It's stone,' she says, 'It went to powder, blew away, left a memory, an image.'

'In war,' I say, 'If that was the cause, you never know where you're situated in it.'

'There's always war,' she says, 'Or simply ignorance. You make things happen, but you don't know why, there is no guide at all through time, through cause and consequence, intention and result – if you are bright, you know, and take precaution.'

'What will that be?' I ask. A kit? A hidden hidey room, unfindable, impermeable?

'You'll know, that's all,' she says. 'While you wait, you could write symphonies.'

'True,' I say: 'A hundred years ago, you might.'

'It doesn't matter, not a bit,' she says.

'It matters to the horses, Sonia,' I say.

They're nowhere, so it must be up to us. To me.

'Suppose it doesn't matter, not a bit. Besides, seeing you standing there, as pale as pale and clueless – what else did they need to know?' she asks: 'They had your number in a twink. No help, no use.'

'Is this what the test's about?' I ask.

'You got it wrong,' she says: 'There are no answers to the test, if there are questions, who knows if there's an answer that is right?'

'Are you New Age?' I ask. 'A Zionist? White Power?' She laughs, and soon I join in too.

*

'You invited all those people,' Sonia says, 'Experts in what surrounds. Knowing there's no room. To spite me? Should I leave? You know I won't....'

'I speak what comes into my mind – I don't romanticise the spontaneity,' I say: 'There's people coming all at once, as it's the only way I have them to stop them coming here in dribs, and needing some attention. This way – they're hugger-mugger, fending for each, for no one else. And it shows. Their culture makes no odds: – they all have funny names and come from everywhere – by leaky boat or donkey cart ... A special limousine, or jeeps. It makes no difference. The same things make them leave from where they came: new ruins. New excavations, and new hypotheses.

'We are a species, Sonia. All gods are much the same, have been, to everyone: the dances too, and sex laws gendered to protect the males, every practice has its twins all round, every recipe ends up in the stomach as anonymous substance, and satisfies the common need.'

'The people you call friends – they could be digital wisps,' she says.

We laugh.

I start to disagree, but she is right. She says, 'They come to see the houses. Those that didn't fall down burnt were submerged. Those – people – that didn't fall down burnt were drowned. An atrocity, or a turmoil? It's curiosity that drives the strangers here and then away to something else. You're just a case – an empty case.

'You are the critical example, forever, not like them. We need to set you upright on a path that leads you to where you know not where....'

'I'll send them on an ibex hunt, to keep them occupied,' I say: 'The animals around – they all drowned, many humans did so too, except that some had understood the mechanics of the raft....'

SHAKE THE BAG. HERE COME THE CLOWNS

'Time.' I say, as people arrive, 'Look, Sonia, what it's done to you. Ruined. And to all the houses, except for mine, and me.'

'Water and fire,' she says: 'It was a designated zone. You were warned, how it would turn out....'

'Not that I'd survive, alone,' I say, 'Or that your body would pay a price – deformed, forgotten.'

'Why ask these jokers?' she asks: she's angry underneath. Her mode is 'therapeutic'. She's stuck in it, until she shapes up and rages out. Gives up, admits she's not of use.

'They're experts in charring and stumps,' I say: 'The houses round, matured, steeped – bones in green sauce.'

'You must feed the experts,' she says. 'You're responsible. Although – you're a fake. Can fakes get more fake as they age, I wonder?'

'We're all fakes, Sonia,' I say: 'We all are instructed. The brightest spend all their lives seeking more instruction, more information. More dependency, and less originality. Did we start off as persons? Not for long. The enlightened can't act, they repeat. Genius defers to dictionaries.

'Only the few raised by wolves have learned from observation and hints. The rest – have their brains electroplated from the start. "Ask, learn; believe what they tell you."'

I open the window, shout, 'Nothing to see here, nothing to see! Move along, move right along.'

The little band falls back, then take this as a welcome. They flit through the trees – the stumps of tree – the water liked it, when the houses had burned away, and it stayed. This house was apart.

So, fire and water – they replace the village – if you want to make a scene, you burn a village, not houses, burn what you think is life. Life sneaks in often, comes again. Crawls and burrows, toadstools and snails. Sometimes to make the point, you have to burn the world.

There would be friends, investigators. Assessors – a team, with tents and bed-rolls, measuring and drawing. I'm the survivor, the witness number one. The experts make a picture, big; much bigger than what there was, in more dimensions.

You can load it in your memory. It will be more intelligent than you could visualise, more potent and more beautiful. Immortal, more or less. A report, the kind that doesn't bang.

'For your eyes only'.

Alone of course, alone at last. The pros, the social types, they call normality a loneliness, more pointedly – a solitude. The 'being by yourself' – as if it's strange! It's not – it's back to where we started. Before the circumstance made us dependent on each other, and lived in compounds, killed the animals, had families that make you anxious, sad, oppressed the women, sent the men to fight in wars.

I invent it all – Sonia, lover and/or therapist; the atrocities that everyone denies, the team of comrades-cum-inspectors – too thorough, picayune, I fear, to sort out good and bad, to find a time when we start counting good and evil actions, reaching a sign that indicates which way to the future, the good, the bad – that says only 'How Far?'

And the guidebook to the world, the universe: 'Worth the visit....' 'worth a detour', 'no lingering'; then 'away, away!'.

The future – lies where the famous ass had no idea, like us, which fork to take. Right or left – is that the choice? Where to? Do we, did the ass, know where?

Don't think about yourself – 'one' can't be a sample of anything. You feel a fool? Many people who don't even dream of one another, took part, without rancour, in doing you down, stripping your tail-feathers: hunting you. It's done to them, to everyone. It isn't good – forget it.

You're not a horse, you weren't burned as an example; not colonised, not a faction boss, a pusher, a fanatic, a seeker after justice, an embezzler – you're relatively pure. 'Pure' means you can be fleeced, with no comeback. You're a resource, though not for you yourself. You're exemplary, a human.

Real people are always with you, even if they've died. It's not a paradox – they talk, they analyse. It does no good at all, but they're not there for that, for doing good, besides, they mostly don't do bad. It's up to you now, all of it.

OLD LETTERS, OLDER STAMPS

Marx was the antiquary, classicist, echt *Westerner – numismatics, mathematics ... Ancient Laws, and Physiocrats. History. History and people were unkind – they did for him. His coffin passed to the East. Engels entertained the peasants: – Marx was with the experts, academics – the intellectuals, the gents. The chiefs. Over there – the dark East, the oriental despotisms. Palmyra, the Arsacids. Huns – why? What profit moved them? Cash? Ransoms? – East is East, you can't destroy it, make it go away. Poor people, barbarians, beyond the reach of intellect.*

Revolution was ordered, placed in an order. The past, the experts – they were wrong – but what happened had to happen; and the future? You could project, shape, deduce it –except ... Bakunin was wrong, disorderly, spontaneous. The magician! Danger! Away with him!

You had to be right – the future was order, reasoned out. What was outside your calculation was an exception: – Russia? Your bastard?

And you? No more a revolutionary? A silver-fish wriggling through a mound of books?

They say Engels was the amateur, the self-educated, who thought revolution was scientific, and nature was dancing to the same tune, a Ländler *maybe – accompanied by artillery riffs. Revolutionary – or was it evolutionary? Or just – everything is nature, us and the others, the residue in fur and plume, going on, forever onward: into the future, the unknown? Welcome! All for the best.*

Good stuff, but there was no evidence, no books, no citations, no lab. Too bad. No finches.

'Yes, Piet, you betrayed. Caution leads you to it. Saved something, not yourself, for sure. No blame. That's what I said, I thought,' says my old friend, who kicks the bottom out of every bucket, every person – '*People are boring, relating to them is dull, if you ever consider it. So you must not. Be for yourself alone, and plough your strip of earth by hand.*'

He wouldn't come along, not with the other experts. It stings, that he finds me boring too. He knows about the archaeology of trees. The only subject not dull, he says.

Still, those two, Karl and Frederick – they were fine old plants. Yews? Old pines? – the fire that killed the horses whipped through them both – left bits of green but the roots were gone to smoulder.

The horses – I couldn't get over that.

The horses were concreteness, for sure. Where does 'the concrete' come from? In our world, there's a common process – abstracts turning into concrete: – despots becoming absolute monarchs ... not determining the system but being determined by it ... Horses becoming chargers, imperial steeds?

Thrones for the little emperors?

Concreteness: – the world, 'everything that is'. And abstraction? Is it 'talking about everything'? Where it all starts and ends – the world. And the abstract? Paradise? Oblivion?

There must be Desire; for us, all is a product of desire, like it or not: – the result's a concrete, surely, what we need to plant our feet on, in this flooded zone. Forward with Desire. What we get is what we want, must want. People cheer. I don't. I don't want to be a Small, desiring a Mister Big ... finding solutions, to *become* Big, like becoming Doktor Caligari, an evil wind who knows your secrets: a universal model, everyone in step, aspiring to be a climber like King Kong ... lover of beautiful women too, you bet ... Can I do it? Call myself out, surrender?

Is my ambition – to be what I am?

You can be an expert on trees, because you aren't one. But – an expert on horses? Maybe you'd be only an expert on their death, like yours. It's the great problem for experts, it all dies, is dead, while you're unpacking your theodolite.

An expert on experts? I hadn't thought of that, but I have now ... Love, being not alone? I consulted the books 'De l'Amour', the 'anti-Oedipus'. A game of love, a drive – desire. People seeping into people, stealing a march, an ambuscade. One tricky joust, even a tricksy one – love. You must be the magus, conjuring a love ever-lasting. Desire? We all have that, it's ours, each of us, alone. Ensconced and independent, autonomous, set inside, the clockwork in a clock. Desire, the coiling of the spring.

Still, thankfully, the experts showed you how to be alone, to choose it, earn it, be condemned – but reaching an altogether higher level of solitude – seeing through everybody, even myself, until all people were a transparent forest of virgin birches. Moving with the winds, silvered. No predator except time. Me – becoming different, more clued up, but utterly changed and yet still me myself. Green or brown. Leafy or stark. Time, the mover.

Trees again. You need never to have seen one, to know it all – though knowing all cannot affect them materially ... it's armchair wisdom, not binding wounds, ensuring futures, building a memorial, turning forests into useful, honourable, pellets.

Once again – which do we trust? Our history, our innovation and our interests? Or our species, struggling in the wearisome unrolling of environments – their heating and refrigeration, sodden lands and fetid seas – a fevered skeleton afflicted by a rash of boils, dead spots and agues, bones that collapse and hands that switch from claws to webs ... Seek wealth or nurture nature? Where's the snare? The switchback? The permanence? The promise.

Living here – it's a bombardment. Bombing's like a story, rather less a poem – there are characters, and there's the right ending, surely, and the protagonists are there, then nowhere; call it 'somewhere'. They are characters – live in the book and nowhere you can call on them. The bomb – is not catastrophe – it's the conclusion of a something else, long as a boa, long as the stretch of sea that's out there every morning until it's on your floor and up your walls.

ALONE

Bombed. They've all gone, like in bombardments.

Flown off, my figments: – Sonia: the friends and experts: the people who knew what was happening and how it would go on. All not here, they were somewhere, and somewhere they must be. And from somewhere you can't disappear, although the cops – they're not much interested; the people with the death stats – they count, and they're sympathetic to tall numbers – but it's clear – the people you used to know and talk to, they've all gone somewhere and you can see where they once lived, the bits of houses, that are like the bits and pieces you failed to put together when you were young – trying to fit the couples together, men with women mostly, usually incongruous and battling; setting them right in place, in a room you once knew but many more you imagined, probably got wrong, and many of them with an animal that made impressions much brighter, clearer, than the people, and they too – all gone. You were told 'get used to it', you were an animal but unlike them. It's not possible: the chicken, the goat, the dog in the yard – they liked you, knew you more deeply than any humans did, certainly more than the family, more than the lovers that you came to have and sought for intimacy in them, from them, that never came, while ... yes, the little cat, the pigeon, they knew you. They liked you, even when you teased them, you were cute then, even when you hurt them – and excused yourself inside because you knew what would be their fate, that it would hurt them much much more and was more defining than anything you could do to them. Your little human playmates? Were acorns, became bushes and trees.

All gone. Bombed, torched, driven away, all of them, their houses uninhabitable, dust and splinters. The memories – I wasn't asked to frame them, file them, I have a pile of them, disordered and inconclusive. Memories, not people. Like numbers, calling cards – all 'unavailable' and disconnected now.

I shooed them off, created them and had them die.

If we wrote history, it wouldn't be like this, a stupid ending, the writer bored and sick, killing us all off before we'd started properly, nothing to describe, all flat and flooded.

I'd have a try, stir it all up – America run by Russians, Russia run by Mohicans. One time, one dream, one order – quite improbable. No one seeking to be loved, or claiming to be really doing what they say they are ... Sovereignty passing to the wondrous beasts. China, India – governed by their monsters. Dragons – the creatures uniting earth and heaven; the monkey armies – resolute, invincible – accepting payment in bananas and those little nuts.

Nothing plural, nothing singular: a story. Experiment and improvise: guess!

This is just a by-blow – the songs, life-long commitments, come and go, and we're still waiting for the big one – the Big One – and hope it will still be Big and memorable, a drama ... fiery angels, the all-consuming fire, hell on earth – if we don't have to wait too long, until it will come, eventually, as a flight of 'Big Ones...', the overpowering storm, with many heads.

There's no sense in this – we're terrified of a future that we've made, we always are, and once there was apocalypse, and now it's secular ... we are lost creatures, exiled from nowhere to create an edge and live upon it....

They killed my neighbours – not for what I'd call modern reasons – but for primitive resentments, needing no explanation to their side, nor to anyone's. Enmity: dislike: hatred: a long slide of provocations and anathemas – beliefs and faiths, theft of land, of horizons, and of identity. Contempt. Phobia. The rage to kill and then the liking of it; shamed, a slow false disavowal of the passion, and the invention of modern policies, procedures, and always the conviction it is right. What is done, is right. Get rid of them, hurt them, then eliminate them. No better rationale, and both sides, when there was the chance, both went ahead. Get rid of them, exterminate.... Or – not like that at all not quite. My friends, neighbours, were delicate and reasonable, anxious to make a truce, and yet – they went. In the spate, under the green fields, the splintered floors they went. I never saw them – their fate was a problem beyond my comment, analysis, solution. It marked a failure, proclaimed, that negated anything I could imagine, or propose.

Guilt, aggression: – like stamping on an ant and then on all of them, all ants, their world ... they're tiny, after all, get in everywhere, eat your food and desecrate your altar. Those people could be your slaves, but they're not worthy, not human....

Steal everything they have, kill their kids, and you can live in peace. Of course, after that – you can't trust any one of them, they're all dedicated to revenge....

A FINE STONE HOUSE

When they built their wooden houses, they cleared the stones they found and passed them on to me. The stone house – could be filled with novelties, trash, left scattered when the other dwellings are destroyed. Maybe the house will be too small for fusion trials – the plasma can reduce the stone to dust – but: rockets to new challenging worlds? Where we might study to make a settlement, make houses, a long house. Like what we left.

Dig up Space – so, leave ourselves, the species, as we are: with better therapies, perhaps. You can't help the planet – look outside! Space is warm – no need for mufflers. Stride out naked in the void. Don't forget the flags.

New climates, with new fruits? All of the best variety, not too attractive but quite nourishing.

There've been theories – theories of us living contented in a dualism – a hot and cold, matter and ideal – a history that's all to come, the present one exhausted, bloomed and faded. You'd need new flexibility, accepting everything without complaint; accommodating, peaceful. Up and down, good-bad. Victory-annihilation. All – as it comes.

'Hypocrisy' – that was the name of what we lived in once and now, riding the possibility of contradiction, we're in the presence of dialectic, of dreaming, entertaining a utopia – of change and re-set of the opposites.

None of this was on the Symposium menu. They thought you can't eat contradiction.

We moderns – we lived with chance, with gambling with each others' life. Steps back and forward and back again, bombs and vaccines, sleep on the street or in the Metropole.

So, the house, which with some care would last forever, given over to new themes, new differences, absences and whatever not – would never fall, but be forever compromised. A 'holding of the line' between what lasts and works and what won't work and doesn't last. Difficult? I guess. You never expect to see the end – life is made short, so that you don't.

New people. Yes! Maybe Chinese, and knowing how I love the Steamboat, special fried rice – Mongolian hotpot? ... 'Hail to the chef!'

'Generally speaking, the people's basic identity of interests underlies the contradictions among the people.' Students of the fortune cookie know that non-antagonistic contradictions come to predominate over antagonistic ones.

And will there be such change? And has it, or another, come, already? Check out the figures.

Those give the winners, but – best performance? The world of spectacle means what differentiates is taste; is cultural level ... those who understand and those who don't. Those who cling to what they've grasped, and those who only sing the songs.

Study the elephants – walking in file. Not intellect in charge, maybe, but memory, and experience. Hope, and a touch of 'follow me, I'm lost: – there's no explorer better you will find'.

Don't do politics? Then, you needn't worry about political rights. Atheist? – then studying religions is destined not to change your mind.

In olden times, the peasant cut himself a flute and played it to the sunset and his animals: the woman of the house and courtyard kept a drawer of costumed dolls she'd sewed.

Now? Buyers and sellers. The resentful up against the vengeful. Interests, nothing more, priorities: they're yours to choose. Back to the Greeks, the *logos* that knows no contradiction – inside. Outside the stockade, just slaves, barbarians, freaks – the horse-men, centaurs, inventions you can de-invent in moments. The old stone house can stand – it stands when you who built it, die and disappear.

Life or death – those are first, apparently non-contradictory, principles.

'Nothing,' I say: 'Really nothing. When you interrogate something, it turns out – stories; no legs to stand on. The only force that holds things up is gravity, and that's the force that throws things down.

'All figures of speech.'

No – there aren't alternatives, it's always just the same – adaptation and opportunism, with theories of how it's not like that, or how it could be different, or was quite other, or will be unrecognisable ... Nonsense. That's why they built the fine stone house. It stands, whoever's in it, and if it is destroyed, you use the stones to build it up again, and, every time, the stones are shaped to make a fine stone house – the same, identical.

Come the water: – each stone a stone-fish, stacked high on one another, a pyramid engulfed cracked open, a tower – a tower of towers, a *taj*, shrine, palace, hierarchy of odd fish, families of flounders – each stone with a wall-eye; a crack, a wrinkle, a shroff-mark in the stone, a mouth! – a libertine's suck, greedy and forever primed, the eye also a mouth.

Against the wall of fish, beware – they're precious but quite flimsy, those chiffons in the chiffonier ... the walls will eat up everything, the pictures, the green girl and the Mona, the chesterfields, the *abat-jours*, ingest the carpets, ... down goes the Qum, flower by flower, the water-garden submerging in the flood. All must swim, compete like they do in Alice's pool of tears, all at salt sea – the creatures pretending to be plants and plants that scutter up the walls like mantis crabs. You must build walls: – those throw them down themselves.

Fish-eyes. Those eyes – reporting back. To other eyes.

It's what you hoped for, no? Recognition. Or exposure. Revelation.

A fine old heap of stones, of eyes, of spies.

Her brother became political commissar of a regiment – shot for disloyalty, or loyalty too much. Good riddance!

I broke the mules. I put together guys who'd tried to break the mules, got broken by the mules.

No, it's no good. Stories should be short, shorter than short fiction. A challenge, broadswords or daggers.

'Good or bad, it won't matter when we're dead'. I wonder if Stalin thought that. I suspect not.

What matters? Everything?

If you're fearful, people ignore you – you're nobody. You can be frightened of what's happened, or be frightened of what will happen. Not both. I'm frightened of the past. You don't have to explain that to anyone – they don't care and don't recognise the names. Fear is like porridge – you have to get up early, very early, to make it properly, and it's there all day. No one wants to wash that huge pan, grey and black scurf round the collar – porridge should be salty, but people prefer to eat it sugared.

I asked 'what am I?' meaning 'what should I do?' A fine stone house – gives me no clue. What am I – who cares? So what? In asking, it's clear I don't care myself.

I'm not a writer – so, should I write about the people round here, who exist, maybe, somewhere – somewhere nowhere you can reach? Writing about them, inventing them – it's not an exercise in having power over them. It's not 'good writing', not refined, convincing.

Power isn't everything – it's everything for those who have it, but those who don't, have something else. Themselves: even dented and broken, plants with boiled roots, in tiny pots. But they don't have power, so, power isn't everything. Yet the people round about, who don't exist, they would resent me writing on them, inventing them. What they want is a trace of freedom, being left alone. They want separation, so they can be themselves – and that is written on the coins – 'freedom, separateness and pastimes'.

Inspiration. I go down to the cellar, half under water – there's broken stuff, thrown down from above, shattered when the stone house fell down and was put together again – once stable, respectable, apparently at ease, that first house. Then, restored: jumpy, self-doubting and askew. No longer part of the array of lofty social towers, but dislocated, disjointed. Stowed in the builder's yard of lengths and bales.

Pots, vases, plates. And forcing up from somewhere inexistent down below, a foundation of broken crocks, all that's left of what's forgotten – handles, shoulders of amphorae, crescents of glass from demijohns.

They could take me off, beat me, lampoon me, put me in the stocks, hung from a pole, electrocuted, driven mad by pop music, a thousand cuts – I would be replete with meaning. That, I understand. Does it matter? If something matters – how far will we go for it? Do I matter because the people I know, I see, and I invent – matter? Is it contagious, the mattering?

I think of elephants. I think of whales, of cats – my bright brothers, sisters. Even, I think of dogs and my distrust of them, that they're so ready with their love and showing it, when I am pawky, much reserved.

And why is everything too late?

VISITING

'Where's the old toad?' I hear: 'This is his hole – it must go down and down until the water turns to steam, and then.... the core?'

It's Bindi. She always leaves a question you can't answer, but *she* knows....

'They stood him upright,' says Farjon, 'And clothed him with a house so's he won't fall.'

I make my entrance, tall on the stoop.

'It's true,' I say: 'I used to be progressive – now I feel there's no back and forth, forward and up.'

'Poor Toad!' says Bindi: 'If you're in eternity, you can't change the clocks, can't make mistakes, redress – there is no register for yes and no, for here and there, nor then and after ... We're here to wind you up again, start the clock....'

'If there's eternity,' Farjon puts in, 'We couldn't know. We can't exist in it. Dead's dead, and time goes on – so ... Nothing saved, and no eternity. Decay's the order, the proof that you're alive. Or dead.'

'That's why we're here,' says Bindi: 'To winkle you out your shell, Piet. See if you are quick – or dead – if you had turned to pearl. How splendid that would be!'

'I'm amazed you and Farjon are still together,' I say: 'I'm together, but I'm one. The others – now dead or running ... Together – in a way ... in the ground, or scooting over it....'

'We're together in a different way,' says Bindi, 'We two. Beyond desire, but all now subject to the will. The wish.'

'We live according to our nature,' Farjon says, 'To Nature.'

'Our *natures*,' Bindi corrects him: 'I keep telling you.'

'Does it stop you having an adventure?' I ask.

'It ought,' says Bindi: 'Prudence is written in. But there is curiosity....'

'Follow my leader,' Farjon agrees, 'Not that there's leaders.'

'If you came to see a rebel,' I say, 'That fire is out. I was never rebellious – I had a plan. It was good. No contradictions – it was the obvious. No one of good will could say 'nay' to it, my plan – except they did.

'Then – everything got knocked down. Or it fell – the law of expended energy, that's for sure.

'What had made it move, was power, and will – the universe. It had been set down in myth: – 'stars are fun.' You make a million of them, each one useless, lonely. Make more and more – until there is an end, a last date coded in ... down it will come, the flames go out – darkness at once, like a clean page, and will and power will set up another up twinkly universe – maybe in a jewel-case, a tip, a landfill – all of us with the same brains as before, perhaps one standard type, but bodies with a thousand legs and seven centimetres long....

'It all depends – on the whim of who might have the will, the power....'

'That's why we're here,' says Bindi, shrugging off her pack, the ground-sheet, tent-poles, dropped on the floor. 'We have the will.'

'I didn't need rebel,' I say: 'No will was required. I told the truth, the self-evident, and they fingered me. Persecuted. It wasn't part of any Plan. I was the easiest mark to hit, and they went on hitting me.'

'The guy had a dream and invented the wheel,' says Farjon, 'They tied him to it and rolled him down the mountain.'

We laugh.

'You must have noticed all the corpses,' Bindi insists: 'Your truth: was it elective or selective? See it, tell it all ... or bits. And the burning ... Where had justice gone?'

'The horses?' I ask, 'I didn't think I'd told you. Corpses? Remember, leave the green tag with the body – green indicates decomposition, so when they've decomposed, they go in the archive, in the book. They're "on the books" as it were. Someone must be bookmaker.... If you let the corpses stop you ... they blow around, like thistledown, a hatch of nits. Ignore the suffering conies or the heroic elks. If they bother you, Bindi, the human bodies – choose another business, go against nature, if you can.'

'The adventure is for you,' says Farjon, ignoring what has gone before: – 'We came to get the account, from you, an old and wandering seeker, of what exactly you have found, and what you might have missed. Your enemies, their ploys, your failings – don't interest us at all. Probably – they've grown up like a picket fence becomes a forest.... Forget the hedging: tell us the truth; what's left.'

'Truth's a funny word,' I say: 'Can you shave bits off, like putting garlic in a salad?'

'You go on about the people round here,' Bindi says: 'They went where everybody goes. The people come and go, and when the houses fall – the people are already somewhere else.'

'There was the war,' I say. 'And the troubled earth.'

'That has no relevance,' she says: 'We were your colleagues and we much admired you. You managed to stay there, doing work ... The war finished, this province went under water. The flood seeped in, stayed.

'You improvised. You said yours was a Plan. Then they tightened up the qualifications needed, and made the oldsters do the test.'

'And so, they made me leave,' I say, 'Defined the terms, and put a term on all of us – the visionaries. Game over! And go a-wandering.... I know – I couldn't do the work. I was quite wrong for it – I didn't want to make it end up where it seemed to tend.... We must all be responsible, for everything. Nothing that happens can be justified ... your work is useless from the start.'

'Work is never done,' says Farjon: 'It's always possible, but always beyond you, and you have to move. You end up where others ended up, they're sent away, and then you are. Or you stay, lamenting that you couldn't do the work.'

'Couldn't do it, wanted not to, was pleased not to do it,' I say: 'Truth and justice – always just beyond my grasp – but following the line my arm was making, you saw quite clear ... the outstretched finger ... ready to write on walls.'

They both laugh.

Bindi has an orange *mèche* – but, the rest of her, it doesn't trend. Both she and Farjon smell of mint – maybe they met the tea-man by the stream. Farjon writes things, pondering, it seems – into an agenda, grey leather cover ...

He must be forty now, brown hair still, but the beard is grey.

'That test!' says Farjon: 'It never ends – each year it's tougher, and you're taken off the list. Put on another one, where you're indelible. The list of the mistrusted. It's unavoidable – the test tests what and who you are – so you can't dissimulate.'

'You can,' says Bindi, 'But you're still you, you're different, that is all. The type you are is permanent – it's why you're tested in the first place....'

'I remember, Bindi,' I say, 'Sending in answers. I did some kind of test myself. Was that my work? or something else, a preamble, a warning or a guarantee? Am I my work? Is my work me? I've seen my thoughts, put on the shelves....'

'A grand old trouper, Piet,' she says, and cuddles me. 'Never a foot put wrong!'

I see she winks at Farjon – colleague? Lover? Everything; a flabby holdall of relationship....

'I studied' I say, 'I thought. You should have looked at it.'

ADVENTURE

'Adventure!' says Farjon, changing his sodden shoes for sneakers.

It rains – it floods. There's torrid heat – the ground is hard, so when it floods the water rages, stays.

'It's wonderful to see you both,' I say: 'And to see you're staying for a good long time. But, as I told you, long ago – you tend to cheapen things. Time doesn't move – it's an illusion that it does – it doesn't dig, expose things, it won't reveal the buried hoard. It isn't reason, so that you can launch in with your spades, just as you please, and find the situation laid out ready, waiting for your intervention, set up and orderly.... finding a past, like us but clumsy, improvised, the gaps filled in by chants and sacrifices ... The past is puppet theatre, complicated, all those rods and strings. Time – is now, exactly what you see today....'

Bindi recalls, 'You said "Time is chaos, History is chaos. People are disorderly, they lie, disguise, they change their shapes, ideas, their looks – they start off sleek and voluble, in tears, in baskets: end toothless, the head razed, deflated ... in cots ..."'

'We wondered how you'd ever find a partner,' Farjon says: 'Sex was impossible, since you thought too long. Bets were taken....'

'You're quoting your conclusions,' I tell them, 'About my work. All I set out was a starting point – of disbelief. A mind that skates on water. The rest was up to you.'

'And it was quite impossible,' says Bindi: 'All you proposed. You used to say, free-wheeling:

'From chaos – there is only chaos, whatever the manual might say. Just think – "experience": always different and unexpected, you shuffle it around, like a joker in the pack of cards. Those cards are meaningless. They stand for what you want, and so – they stand for nothing.'

'Everybody wants to win,' Farjon puts in. 'Then, they lose, don't care ... don't win.'

'That's what I came to think,' I say: 'It wasn't what I wanted. Winning – always the come-on: beauty, precision ... it doesn't mean you've won anything, anything substantial. All prizes – consolation.

'The suffering – however much you turn away – is part of you....'

'Isn't that a mysticism, Piet?' asks Farjon: 'Not you at all!'

'What *is* you, Piet?' asks Bindi, with half a laugh: 'You were a champion of progress, and also the theorist of the hole that trips the mount.

'We have a theory too. You suffer, suffer isolation so you can hide what you don't want to see, want nobody to see. And yet – it's out there, everywhere, traduced and lucid: – reality. A pack of it, realities, like bison, or alpacas. Yours to choose the version. What you see as truth....'

'Is like the Victory of Samothrace,' adds Farjon: 'A harpie, headless and magnificent. The scythes and pistols once she held – have dropped away, somewhere along the road.'

'The paper,' Bindi says: 'That was the truth. We made it come out every day and by the dusk – it wasn't there ... Used to light fires, wrap cod, or hung up in the outhouses, in squares unreadable... "For your bum's eye only". Forgotten, dirty, and unloved. And anything you put in it, Piet – needed to be not only true but *all* the truth....'

'You're wasting time,' I say: 'Of course, it never was like that. It was the truth, and *not* the truth – surely you knew? I always did. You should have challenged me, and risked being known – as reactionaries, stoolies, agents of another truth, a falsity ... except....'

'Except you hoped that time would set you right, make up for what you never could,' says Bindi ... 'And prove the sceptics wrong, except ... for you. Some hope! You flew that kite....'

'We all do,' I say: 'Truth is constructed, just like hope. There's truth, and there is history. You can have the truth about the chaos, or the truth about the hope. The choice is yours.'

'That's rather what we thought,' says Farjon, and puts away the small grey book.

'I am here.' I say, 'Valuable, in my way. Unsaleable. But, there are shards – search them, the shards. You might go down and find a "chicken bowl", or something else, looted and really valuable – that could make your fortune if you sell, or reputation if you give it back. Or – there are simple shards. If there's no restoration, there is history, a tale, invented ... how the shards got here, survived, shattered. And remember – the alternative is always worse. The enemy is always worse, worse than your side. There is always an alternative, it's your opponent – you do your best to counter it.

'Alternatives are part of chaos, nothing more – but they exist – against the worse, you struggle. Struggle is not truth. Maybe you're wrong? The cosmological eye – perhaps it's purblind? Too bad – if there is truth, there must be lies, and being wrong ... and better you to see the lies, the truth, than wander on believing what you want, or what is easier, or harder, to believe. It's quite irrelevant, what you believe. But – it's always better to be lucid when you set out on the curving stony road.

'Drunks? They sit by your path, and offer plays and ploys, and tell you jokes. Is that your interest? A poem or a little play – the drunks are good at heel-and-toe, and roundelays – they make you laugh and cry, that is their trade. Don't drink from their flask – it's gall.'

'You wander off,' says Bindi: 'Piet! Attention! Forget the drunks and mountebanks.'

'It's been destroyed – all the houses; I'm deprived of any future, I barely have a voice, and there is no one listening anyway. This is the alternative, the worse; what you call suffering,' I say.

'There is no meaning here,' Farjon says: 'What you are, and think and see – it doesn't mean a thing, it doesn't matter, not a bit, the view from this stone house – what does it signify? The truth? A view. The windows – they could all be blocked, with fine old stones – or paint the walls with scenes of green and shepherd dogs. Don't look out – there is no story here. Eyes closed: – and think!'

'An adventure will bring the light to you, Piet,' Bindi says: 'For you and on you. Think of it as revolution. It's not dissimilar – full of episodes when, notwithstanding chaos all around, there were alternatives much worse. How do you face those down ... cheer everybody on?'

'You mock me, Bindi, but that's not a punishment,' I say: 'I am curious – what's the test? An adventure is a test, a real one, without therapy, without assessment. No one fails ... most don't return.'

'The people in the houses, who were they?' Farjon asks: 'Did you bother to find out?'

'They were nomads who went on to found a civilisation. Or found one ready-made,' I say, 'And were its human core. Listen. Forget radicalism, revolution. Those happen, wax, wane. Illusion, hope, despair: – bad conceptualisations. No definition, no fixed meanings.

'Power and individuals – the past. Come to terms with it – the power, the past – that's made you as you are.

'Fit things together, fit together masses of disparate things, and dip them in civilisation. That is all that matters – the rest is journalism. What is indelible – is never spoken about. The flood – is unmistakable – it shapes my life, I can't walk outside, can't have a dog, probably not a cat. I shout about that all the time. But civilisation – I have mine ... Civilisation? It was huge, it was the world, everything that is, civilisation – it was all I – anyone – had, so of course, that would bury you, or you would bury it. All there is: – reality. Take your brush, and paint it – differently ... how could it be "different"?

'The adventure – won't even take an afternoon. It means you think you'll live a long long life, longer than is ever recorded, living it, living it up, and into, your own self ... you're probably a demi-god, nearly an immortal ... and then you see, you're wrong, too late. You're moribund!...

'Adventure: you can have it because of civilisation. It's ephemeral, but you put a foot outside your comfort, your home and castle. You bet you can get back afterwards, to your security. Security is civilisation, which must be promulgated, shown and demonstrated – by love. Even against your wish – you love it. You must – you're in it! It can be improved – all lovers, objects loved – can be improved. Whoa! Steady! Love – too strong? Friendship, let's say: or empathy. Tone it down, for sure. You must embellish it...

'Give it presents – even a punch. Art, my friends! If your world stinks, turn it into something odourless. Art! That's how I thought, I think....

'War can spread your civilisation, but the people, dead or subjected – can only accept your civilisation if there's love... Affect, say. Idealisation? ... Indifference even. You and them: if possible, in love. Hostility – ends in war, civil war. Or revolution: – a symptom that something has failed, and needs to be repaired, built up.... changed entirely.'

'Well!' says Bindi, amazed: 'And civilisation – do you have it here? Let's agree – what knocked this neighbourhood to mud – it can't be civilisation? But then, what is it, do you have it? Expect to have it? How much sugar did you take? Or are you fooling?'

'We're back at the start,' I say: 'First it was "revolution". It didn't make the change, the change of everything ... Now – civilisation. We know this isn't it, what we have now. We know, that no one wants this world, its low highs, abyssal lows – though it is true, that even chaos must have shadings, some tolerable states, some – grand macabre. And some a devastation ... Civilisation – you must believe it can be changed, transformed – or else you wouldn't love it, live within it, hope it can be transformed ... tolerate it.

'Or – maybe after all, it *is* about power, and all and only that. Chaos is survival, duration, and it's death as well. Death lasts longer, but survival perceives time, rides on its back. A circuit.

'Who whom? Up or down, on top or underneath? – that is the concrete and the abstract too. Remember Ur – the soldiers carrying severed heads of other soldiers, a radical choice, where once they cut off feet, cut hamstrings, to make the captives useful slaves. The answer, in the end is – death. Not compromise, not cruelty, nor "hoe that row". No. Death.

'Alas, the leopard, *nimrum*, hunted to extinction, with the honours of the fallen.... potential friend, now skinned, a rug.

'You can fit me into that, you two.'

They step back, and I hear 'Another con!' says Farjon. 'The old toad, the flittering fox – we'll never catch him. When he's toad, he takes the contours, colours, of a hole. When he's the fox – he's a red leaf, a fallen frond. First "revolution" – we can't pin him down on that. Now – "civilisation". Another scam? Another labyrinth. Liberalism, when it's already died? Democracy, now the bad guys run it? Or tribalism, when the world is made of continents at war?'

'He's skittering away, that's clear,' says Bindi: 'We won't catch him, he's a mayfly – reborn in every daily swarm – quite indistinguishable from all the other flies, even his human face erased.

'And are we wrong to think he's always an original?'

'Surrealists thought we were all originals: – quite unique, our dreams interpreted, but never shared. It isn't so,' says Farjon: 'There's a stock set of them, our dreams. The faces change, the situations don't.'

Why, really, did they come, those two?

Farjon takes photos – do we trust the camera? Spying with fishy eyes – a tug at the heart, at the sleeve. Alpacas – first farmed, then preserved – away they run, into the land of freedom, skinned, stuffed and shafted ... into carts. The past – captured, frozen – makes you cry and laugh, but after all – gone, dead.

Over the mountain, there are mines: – rivers diverted down the plughole, now washing someone's smalls – the miniature silent motor cars, they need the sludge to power them up – now you see them, now you don't ever hear them ... traffic with the drivers all enclosed and silent, no caravans, no wonders; the glass, ceramics – all in pieces, dropped off the camel's back, down in my cellar....

The people, yes! Bindi will step in – won't save the river and the frogs; the corporation sinks the mine, but the people ... she will save those, get a percentage from the poisonous diggings ... make the owners up their price. It's goodness: – I don't want to live there now, but for sure, it's good for them, those sad sad people. Maybe I don't want 'good', never have, don't recognise it, happy in the dirt, the bad, the improvised, the unexplored, unmapped. Resentment, not revolt or transformation?

'Look up,' I shout: 'Look up, higher than the mountain – see what's lodged above you! Forget the river – don't drink the water, it's made of gold, it'll plump you up, the fat goose full of golden eggs ... constipated ... Look up at the big silence, mooning above you, don't switch it on, don't try to make a word out of its mountains – I know you can't ... You've got this far, you know it's soundless, my taradiddle, it won't plug in, won't receive, compute – but....

'But look! The hole is there, watch it! You've fallen in already, did you get out? I've no idea.... You're under a big power, it presses on you, oppresses – you empty out your lungs, you're full of iron braces, your belly is a rusty cage, and every breath inflates the despot, a thousand times puffed up, and with a face ... yours? Not mine, for sure. The Spirit that brings Cargo sends you out, armed with a bamboo spear, to prick your brother? Or your boss? Nothing works, except your tears – they wash the gold dust off.... be satisfied, they're truly yours, no one can cry for you, do it in silence ... You need the despot – where's it gone? Can't you invent it? No, of course not – it's indispensible, and fortunately – it's not there. Nowhere. Like air – you don't see it, but it makes you live.

'The despot's coming, though. Everywhere. Is it you? Bindi, is it you?

'You can't absorb. What you absorb, you can't expel. You're in a bind! Look up into the void – and whoa! You've fallen in the hole.

'You know the easy answer – I just told you! Don't gamble on the absences....

'Farjon is lost,' I tell Bindi: 'I need nothing, nothing for myself, and there is no one round about, no one who'd profit from what I have.'

'It's all broken, Piet,' she says: 'Farjon's looking for things to sell. Old, broken things. I despise that, but I love him. You've nothing whole. Not you yourself. I want a picture – a picture of a tower much taller than your piddling fine stone house – with a despot. A despot who's a voice. Loud and bright. Funny.'

'It's all quiet here,' I tell her: 'I'd have loved to have a cat, but with the water round – where would she hunt, roll in the dust, or meet her suitors?'

I know – Bindi wants a noise, a voice, to talk with, against. Practise with it, till it's hers, it's her. She wants the power to prove she is alive.

'Do you think your despot wants to talk?' I ask.

'Historically ...' she says, 'Despots leave runes, and piles of stones. Crumble. Impressive, just like we'd like to think we leave behind – but broken, partial – the jewelled eyes gouged out, the eternal laws and revelations looted ... the fragments buried in the sand, in cellars, undeciphered, ignored. The voice – it should be young and powerful. It doesn't matter, so long as it's loud – and I'd not expect a private chat ... there's millions of me, each with a signal, switched on....'

'War is noisy, Bindi,' I say: 'Dull and stupid too.'

'Unfortunately,' she says, 'You're not the despot everybody wants. Am I? Could be!

'You talk, but don't reverberate. We want a voice, coiled in our brain, as fresh and crispy as a bamboo shoot, green and white –

that tells us what to do, the rules, the penalties, what friends and parents might have done and said that we should do.

'The laws, Piet: the voice that has to tell us what is what because it dies when we do, becomes the maggot that rears up and croaks the moment that we do. Too bad! But we must be told. You have to know it all, so you can survive.'

'I didn't tell you, Bindi,' I say: 'I alluded. You weren't to be trusted with a voice, a loud voice, in a language that you didn't recognise. You and Farjon – like the rest, making it all up, and being dissatisfied because you knew – when you were alone and in the dark, it was invention.'

'What isn't invention, Piet?' she asks.

'You see?' I say: 'Within – you're bright. Brighter than Farjon who wants to snap the animals, and sell the prints ... and someone else will buy the animals and pack them in a horde, sell them in lots, and on and on, until there is enough that we can say "we have preserved what was in danger" and then. And then?'

'Oh,' says Farjon, butting in: 'Those fucking horses. A miscalculation. Accident. No one wants what can't be tamed, confined, displayed. A danger to themselves – intolerable to all the rest. Fatality, or destiny.

'Picking winners, Piet? Me, Bindi – or you? Chance: – you don't know what will win the race, but only one is capable. All the rest, bar that one, are failures, there to keep the pace. Never to win: impossible. You know that, and without you – it's certain all the same. Ever, only one. The rest – the field – at best a consolation, but, to be frank – merely "the field", the beaten others: all the also-rans.'

'You could leave them be,' I say, 'Not tempt fortune. Leave everything alone.'

'Maybe with animals,' he says, unconvinced – 'But humans? Is that what you think?'

FARJON

'It's always "humans",' Farjon says: 'We've no other choice. We're us. The animals – they come from far away – do they know far and near? Are they geographical, or do they creep and roam?

'Do they love us, fear us – and do we stroke them, cage them, cherish them and eat them? Smash their skulls?

'Of course we do. Them – and us, each other too. We make distinctions, but in the end ... there is the wall. You have to build one, to hold things back, to keep you in, and safe, the others out. Postponing death.... always, you adjudicate, gamble: risk, cross lines ... so, the wall is vital, though it doesn't work.'

'You make pictures of them, Farjon,' I say: 'You exploit the animals, except – it isn't really so. You exploit us. You take the pictures, sell the pictures. People will pay to observe them, animals, except – it isn't them; it's the apparent beauty of your pictures that's the prize. Our aesthetic, not their life. They pay to adopt an animal – it doesn't move, they aren't its mother, or its grannie.... The tie's ephemeral ... A picture – seems truly to belong to you: permanently....'

'I'm in the picture business, Piet,' he says: 'The animals – better for them not to exist, not to depend. And then – we have a favour to ask of you.... or, it's a favour that we offer you. The fine stone house – let's say the people come, they lodge, they stare and gawp, they pay to make a picture of themselves – create and buy, buy the best, most beautiful, that includes themselves ... and....'

'Observing me, my fine stone house, for them, I'd be a frame,' I say. 'I am the patriarch who holds the bank. Or – they picture me, and I'm the picture that they take away, me ... I'm silent ... Since it appears I can't be Bindi's voice.... too soft....'

'No,' Farjon says: 'The favour to us isn't to use the house, your house; it's that you keep your silence. The favour that we give to you – is ask you nothing. Be the landscape. Not a word.'

'That's one favour, Farjon: only one,' I say: 'I don't see exchange. I give you everything ... and you? You set the stage, the scene – you reap what? Cash?'

'Pictures,' Farjon says: 'And you can be in one of them. Or even – all.'

'They're miniatures, Farjon,' I say: 'Rocks are more varied, larger. And the ghosts, all round ... Alpacas. Little brush wolves. Silver foxes, clueless without snow. Parrots that have dulled, and gotten small on the trek.... No horses.

'The picture, the book, the sheet of coloured paper – is nothing. No meaning, no life. Probably no death: nothing to mourn, to touch, no words, no cry. No eye to look, no eye to see.

'I couldn't agree, to take so much, beauty and truth, from what is small, and so abrupt and fleeting ... so quiet; so nothing.'

'They're to hang on walls, those pics, so that the walls don't seem like walls,' says Bindi.

'You think it's civilisation – but you lard what you have with dress-up cast-offs, travesties, disguises ... stifling, concealing. It's horrible,' I say: 'All art, the books, the pictures, poems, music – all horrible, like offal from the slaughter-house, scraped off the floor. Scruffs and dead eyes, put in the pickle-jar. All most foul, the dead reflection traded as the thing, thing in and for itself, the spirit skewered, decking a religion. The dead goddess laden with her attributes ... she too gets hung on walls – chiselled in the niche; garnished with the martyrs, the grotesques... Parishioners impoverished to have stone virgins wear a lapis stole... all art....

'You two, reduced to that, to trade in it and fish me in?

'It's balance – between the love there is for what you have, belief it can be changed. Concealing its deficiencies. Change, change utterly, using the people that there are – the wretched of the earth. You know catastrophe would bury everything and everyone, as it always does. And it will come.'

'All we need from you, Piet, is your silence,' Farjon says, 'Holding still,' and Bindi adds, 'You've reached that stage all by yourself, Piet.... you didn't want to talk, to seek help ... No crime, nothing to be condoned or lied about? No penance is required. You're clean – you cleaned youself.'

*

'You know, Bindi,' Farjon says: 'I want this house, the stones, the wall-eyes, I want to climb up to the broken roof and stick my head out and see what Piet no longer sees, probably never even thought to look for ... all the plain; up to the mountains, all the yellowing plants, the movements through the maize, the Indians' corn, gone to seed and again, again, gone to seed and sprouting clowns' hair, fright wigs, the slender animals running through. That's what I want – the house that couldn't fall, despite the failures, the temptations, the only house that stood. My dream house....

'Discipline, Bindi. Conviction, when there's nothing to convince, no object, only me. Subject; seeing everything that moves across the plain, and doing nothing, nothing whatever to prevent what's happening, safe to contemplate catastrophe – protected by these thick brown walls.... All that happens, the quirks, the horrors – all happening outside, to be ignored....'

I hear Farjon shouting, prophesying.

'Hey,' I say, I'm here, still here. Still in my house.'

'Oh,' he says, 'Fear nothing. I won't get in your way, won't even see you, once I'm in. Won't hear you, smell you, watch you, as you age and thin out, disappear.'

'There's empires out there,' says Bindi: 'If you would ever look, Piet.'

'You're right,' I say: 'There's scores, if not hundreds. Which attracts? Empires based on faith or science? Then which? All gods, or just one God? A gene, or the whole mechanism? Genes are a package – you'd need lots to make each of us look quite like the other. Show me! I'll think about it and get back to you. Each is magnificent, no doubt, but flawed and vulnerable. It all boils down.'

'To what?' she asks.

'To what is close at hand. To our own civilisation, our "empire of empires" that is proclaimed anti-imperialist, and yet is always "the Empire" to crown them all... "the World"!' I say.

'Think back to "before" ... everyone round the camp-fire, eating bland food. Modest. Early to bed and late to rise – won't make you wealthy but will make you wise....

'An answer? To respond to stasis, resolving past and present in a future that you think you've found set out already, here and now.

'Those old photos – snow everywhere, because the light got in. Put them back – into the dark. They show how we used to look – up there, in space. We've been on the moon for centuries – Babel Tower – it got up there, only – the elevators inside didn't work. Nobody tells you, why should they?

'I've always been a plodder, an eccentric. My poor rickety cart, laden with true believers, forever winding up their fob watches, onions, they were called – that made them weep! Consulting time? Without the context – only minutes and seconds; time stuck, like fried eggs on the rocks. Those time-pieces need a tea-party to make them tick... Waiting for a happening – anything at all that moves ... waiting for days and years....

'True communism. Remember that?'

'In fact,' she starts. 'No one does. It's good.' She goes ahead –

'I believe, believe in burials – the royal tombs, the sacred cemeteries – those are the best part – leave them be ... The rulers ruled – they're dead and gone: everybody should be satisfied. No resurrections. Use your imagination, not your spade.

'And when you were in the cart, who was your horse, Piet? A true real horse? Or a coupla guys in khaki suits whose legs bent the wrong way? And you, a-top, wielding the knout?'

'No, Bindi,' I say, 'I was the one behind, who pushed.'

'A classic,' Bindi says, 'Supporting role. Nothing you must regret. You're not reactionary, you say – but want to save the civilisation everybody's in, and hope your efforts make it end up radical, transformed....'

'It's not like that,' I say, irritated: I side-step – 'What is a fault, a crime? What's the charge against me? There is a law? A law that makes the crime – or, turn-about – the crime that makes the law.

'The law is what breaks you – you must break the law, although – it won't break like you do. Watch your back – the law can break it....

'People were sent out to the lawless fields – together with their free will, and destiny, making History. Their free will absolves me, cleans me, like a detergent. I'm not responsible for anybody's fate. I knew the hazard comrades went to face – the despotisms: Oriental, African, European and American ...

'Condemnation for a thought, a book, a pamphlet ... a conversation, insult ...? You got caught – with a subversive thought!

'They carried loads; I used an atlas. Victims, ingenuous: a sacrifice? Off they go, to jail, to torture.... Their free will absolves me, the teacher, the despatcher.

'But is it so, that I've no fault, and no responsibility? I sent them off – their mission mine and theirs. They often ended bad. I feel the guilt, but we did no wrong ... no one of us. We wanted good. Did anybody else?'

'A spiritual journey, pilgrimage,' she says, amused and unconvinced – 'It does you good. Like taking a big dog that pulls – out for its walk.... that ends up escaping – going home, where all began, and where it lives.'

'You're right,' I say: 'I don't convince – you wonder, do I convince myself? I don't ring true. I look like silver, but I have a copper core. Maybe it's lead. There is no remorse, no possible vindication, no redemption. Only – sadness. And long long times to think it over.

'And, after all – not to act, even to renege, pretend, be neutral – it is much much worse.'

'It's all past, forgotten,' Bindi says: 'Now, we watch the water, and the bombs – the heat: – all these are malaises that the therapists can handle. Your crime, your guilt, your raptus – doesn't interest. No one remembers. It's like your old coins – they represented power! And now – they're inert and curiosities, and nothing more....'

*

'It's all made up,' she tells Farjon: 'He's not as old as he implies, he's had no power, and so, alas, he's not responsible for anything.

'To feel guilty and have done important things – you need to be a principal.

'Inventing history and moulding time to fit – you'd have to be an artist.

'"If only", and "as if" – for him, those are the provinces of meaning ... Piet and his story – false confessions, wishful guilt, desire for punishment, forgiveness, pardon: – starting anew. A wallow in exaggeration ...?'

'It will have been the horses,' Farjon says: 'It must be so.'

WE SET OUT....

to cross the plain. We disappear beneath the fronds, the yellow sea, infertile corn.

'The plain was barren,' I say, 'Before, you looked out on sand, outcrops of grey. There were blue streams – cobalt or lead? Monitors, chameleons, forever on the run and hide, some scrubby grass. Someone planted corn, a vast extent: they cleared the emptiness with fire ... burnt umber the result ...

'There is no harvest,' says Farjon: 'These plants are barren. Corn like this reproduces when there are male and female plants. These plants are male ... a screen. Maybe we could smoke the leaves. Maybe ... whoever – they didn't even want the corn ... just fronds ... seeking a high....'

We defer to Farjon, Bindi and I, in silence.

'Beyond the mountain,' Bindi says later, 'May be a plantation, females only. Plants too'

'Or – new people coming in, with faith in plants?' I speculate: 'Or two bands of people, each with a useless monopoly in something, some blind faith.... under gendered flags, in donkey carts....'

'The plants can do it all themselves,' says Farjon: 'It depends how they see their chances – in environments they can evaluate....'

'I've never been beyond the mountain, Farjon,' I say. I hope his interest might be seized, so he forgets the fine stone house, and has us go a-voyaging. 'Beyond its foot, that is.'

'What can they be waiting for?' asks Bindi: 'Lizards. Plants.'

'These lizards,' I say: 'They're very large,' and mostly red, purple and black.

There's thousands of them we can see, all turned towards us, watching, mustered. The plants stand close together too ... The monitors' eyes that follow our advance are cool and arrogant....

I touch one by mischance – its skin is warm, is hot.

'They have a scheme,' says Farjon, 'It's going very well for them.'

It's undeniable. Each straddles its plant – not to eat or scavenge off it ... to ride it, like a patient nag.

'What can they drink?' Bindi wonders, 'If they live here, not just passing through.'

'It's unsettling,' I say, 'Because we know so little of what arrives, surrounds us.'

Farjon lifts one off – a fine purplish one, a scarlet crest: it clamps on his bare forearm. He uses the free hand to sketch it, in the grey leather-covered notebook

'The fine stone house – it has no plan, it's completed, you could say it's dead,' says Bindi, rounding her eyes and rolling them: 'Instead – *these* things seek a destiny.'

'It's life they want,' says Farjon: 'Survival. Getting high on leaves, then sex on one another. Don't be surprised, don't exaggerate ... Everything has a plan. Even we do. Get to the mountain!'

'These creatures,' Bindi says, 'Look at them, try to guess what's in their minds. They're what you see when you get woozed on pills, and now – they stare us out! Who knows what they expect? An empire – could give destinies to follow, remedies for many things, and yet....

'An empire always means the species is on a roll, a ramp, and then it always chooses the catastrophe: the fighting to stay top and arrogant. Species supremacy, no surrender! Defeat inevitable ... All empires die so that a new one can be born, over and over ... will it ever end, the cycle? Bigger, more violent, including the contradictions ... that is the model, and in the end ... The End.'

'All states are empires waiting, eager, to be born,' I say, ' – so, we're all expectant imperialists, all in states, and registered. Our destiny is an empire of the empires – all the big empires aspired to that, and on, on we go. Willy-nilly. Too late? No, for empires, lateness doesn't feature – time for one last massacre is always on our side, one last atrocity, a hypocritical lament – all progress, all technology, all future, is a fall-out from production of the industries of war.

'And now, look! Just look! The lizards. Look closely at what they want to be and what they will become.... A million years of reptile power, or tiny green and brown survivors, lodging in the keyhole?'

They've drifted off, Bindi and Farjon. I see Farjon is still fixated on my house – the emptiness attracts, the possibility of filling it with stuff he's made his own, thick windows, doors with bolts, the cellars drained dry as bones, and filled with bottles – fizzy celebration wine.

I think – all's changed – steps forward, back, a falter – down, into the pit, and no! The rich still on their ramp, all round betrayal, lightness of word and heaviness of deed – my motto 'intellect and style' much ridiculed ... The stone house – heroic witness? But of what?

I say to Bindi, Farjon, pointing towards the house – 'A fort, a fortress? But – it's not. It's a stump, the last tooth with no fellow that could make a bite. Look out across the plain, those tall mountains – huge, imposing, promising, concealing – what? Nothing, nothing at all.

'Nothing for you, Farjon, ... nothing useful to coax Bindi back, to make a thorny mismatch with her, if you'd thought....

'Watch them, these reptiles, with their crop.... A horde, that feeds, that prospers, on a nullity ... The fine stone house – a look-out tower, but nothing more.... no refuge, and no monument....'

We push on through the desiccated plants. The big lizards – they don't seem to defecate, nor yet to nibble at the leaves, just wait.

It's very hot. We all hallucinate. Or, maybe – it is only me.

I wave a finger at a beast, and it spits back. Waggles its tongue, and tries a syllable. I giggle, set Bindi off.

I'm thinking of the lady, ''mid the alien corn....'

'Come on, you guys,' Farjon calls out, pushing on, shaking the stems, so that some lizards lose their holds – 'They're small, unarmed. All they can do is stare.'

It's true. They're not a threat. They have their certainty, that's all.

'If we make it to the mountain now,' I say, 'With all this foliage – we can't look back and see the old stone house. We'd have to climb – we're not equipped ... we need a drone, to show what lies beyond....'

'Stop!' says Bindi: 'The reptiles and the plants – they're thinning out. We're through! The expedition carries on – look back, forget the fictions, the surmise, everything we've plodded on. The light! The view! Horizons.... let's enjoy!'

Why do things happen, can we make them happen, and if not ... the suffering, the evil – those happen but there's no explanation for them, no role ... and yet ... the pleasure in the view? What use...?

'Thinking,' I say: 'No use at all. If analysis was any good, all would have been resolved millennia ago...?'

'That's why my plan is "trying something else",' says Bindi: 'You're fucked up, Piet, and you spread it like the 'flu.'

'I'm making final reckonings,' I say: 'Russia – a great conquest, then a loss, a disappointment and a liability, a once grand ally in waiting for the peoples otherwise unknown, neglected ... then? Hmmmm. Things turn into their opposites, and carry on and on, until ... there's something or there's nothing happening. Opposites and continuity – surprises round the corner too. Watch!

'And you'll go goading on. Yet, you'll underestimate old Marx, two centuries ago, and still – the wit, the criticism ... unsurpassed, it seems ... Intellect? And style? Some prevision too, you must admit....'

'You have the house, Piet,' Farjon says, uninterested: 'While everything falls down, or is bombarded into grit – the house can always be repaired ... Intellect and style, you say? That's what you'd use? The species – hatches and swarms: – they can't survive, or understand, thick clouds of alien abundance, like what will come ... Bugs, Piet – will drive you out and level everything.'

'How I agree,' I say: 'It's difficult and quirky – intellect won't save me, nor save anyone. For the house – it's cranes and cutting edges that are needed, to stand it up when it's thrown down.'

'Nothing, in other words,' says Bindi: 'You've no defence. No style, no intellect. You just wait and see.... Everyone was right to fear you: – what did you want – a despotism or an anarchy? Dictatorship or an immense plurality? Gangs, elites? Cops, robbers?'

'Probably,' I say: 'Everything of that – according to the circumstance, which we couldn't recognise, still less control.

'Your "nothing", though. What functions in those novel circumstances you don't recognise, still less control. You wait and see: enthusiasm, interests – you have them all. Wait! It's all a mystery that keeps you on the hop! But wow! It gets resolved, and quick: resolved by force – and you're the field-mouse beneath the harrow, if you don't find some new strategy ... Do you have that?'

'Does everyone?' asks Bindi: 'Perhaps. Not me. What I want, I work out for myself, and act alone:– there's no one talks or argues.... On, the powerful drive, with what they have decided ... That leaves free space – it's where Farjon hopes to bunker down, in the house that isn't his.

'And probably, Piet – not yours.'

'Don't preen, Bindi,' I say, 'And Farjon – don't insist.

'Another day – we'll make it to the mountain foot, and try to climb. It's a volcanic mound ... consider well, if curiosity drives beyond the safety bar, endangers us beyond our hopes....'

'I should tell you,' Bindi interrupts, 'About the house. We've nowhere else to stay. We don't do anything that's useful, so we don't have work, or cash.'

'Of course,' I say, 'I realise. No need to insist – there's many of us who have long since not produced, and wait for things to happen to us.... I'm the lucky one – I have the fine stone house ... I don't intend relaxing my life-sustaining hold on it, no, not at all....'

'You're slippery,' says Farjon, losing patience: 'A loose cannon. At least, it's clear what a cannon's for, and what it does. You, instead....'

'When you arrive,' I say, 'At a point you can't go forward ... and the whole system, when there's no way anyone could mend, restore it ...then ...!'

IT'S STILL

very early – the nights are cold, the dawns are rigid. We see what seems a tall ice *stupa* – set in a clearing where there are no stems of corn ... 'It's Mister Whippy,' Bindi says, in awe: 'Without the sex.'

'A green ice, pistacchio, with peppercorns, or blueberry pips set in ...' says Fajon, equally in wonder.

'They're eyes,' I say: 'Nothing they can see, until the sun comes up. This heap – the lizard bodies, stacked in a pyramid, their colours lost, everyone this pale green, a gelid huddle ... When the heat comes on, they regain their colour, the whole stupa will unstick, unfold, and they'll take up their platforms – until then, this dark light-house will preserve them cuddled tight....'

And it is so. As the plain warms, the ice-mound melts, the reptiles peel away and hit the ground, they scuttle off – they blush to red, lilac, and purple, egg-yolk and daffodil, take up their stations on the corn. It's a sign, an absence: if you would be dominant, you must be vigilant, awake all day and night.

'It's marvellous,' says Bindi: 'Like those Amerindian cities – a fort of earth, a worm-hill rounded, burrowed out inside – a *métro* of corridors and sneak-holes ... where humans toted loads, made moulds for sacred figurines, executed prisoners, blew bamboo trumpets, boiled up the stucco in clay cauldrons.... calculated the azimuth, and eclipses of all stars, visible, imagined – planets like a flight of Stetsons tossed high up – inhabited or dry and wrinkled like cold omelettes.... – ah, Piet,' she shouts, 'The mathematics! These first cities – were the best ... most intricate, an ant-heap of togetherness and mutual aid, perishing by over-heating or by forgetfulness, by ratiocination excessive – those equations, the calendars, the syzygy – too beautiful, seductive... awaiting gods from other universes, courteous and swathed in silk, alighting from their dog carts and their jaunting-cars....

'... But the sewage, Piet, the fevers, rubbish ... the fruitful earth, turned to a monstrous heap of shit....'

The lizards – do they calculate? They surely must, there's nothing else if they want to be the boss. And – they don't defecate.

'The mountain,' Farjon says, pointing a long spyglass at its top – 'There's steam. And flame.'

'I know,' I say: 'It's a volcano, on a fault. It happens like that over and over, always the same, the outcome always different. A massacre, then new land and islands born, settlements – destroyed or set in aspic. Eruptions – like a curtain coming down – and see! The scene has changed, the cast, the actors, all replaced.... Over and over, the same and different each time, it's something you can't stop up, can't put a bung on the fire and expect that will extinguish it.'

SONS AND FATHERS

Farjon strides ahead – Bindi and I, we struggle after. The sulphur gets into our lungs, our legs. The mountain steams and squirms.

'Farjon,' I say, on impulse, 'You're disagreeable enough to be my son. Seeking arguments – seeking my shell, my house, hoping I'll go down – into the hot-spot, a fissure, down in the pot, the roiling kitchen, the saucepan where they broil the stones ... Then – orgasm, and up it goes – the pumice and the poison, and down it comes – the black bile....'

'You didn't build the house,' he says: 'It was built round you. It's your armour, your skin and scaly itch – your coffin.'

'Nothing is transmitted,' I tell him: 'We start off strangers, and on we go, strangers in the stage-coach – shooting from the windows, robbing each other; and straining on, the horses race – and we turn grey and hard, we lose mobility, we end with sticks to hold us up, and then – we are the sticks....'

'You were born old,' he says: 'Full of old ideas – like the youth who thinks he'll do what his father tried, and failed – to climb, to bring it back ... the albino animal that talks, the long long sword, the maiden: in her naughty nineties now....'

'It wasn't up to me,' I say: 'Intellect and style – they're yours, or else they're not, they're not bequeathed in any case. They're all I have, and they were not inherited.

'When I was very young, I did a tour – to see first cities, the pyramids, the snakes, the jaguars – the little sacred bird. A train broke down, a single track – so, we ran off, into the fields in case there was a collision, another train headlong and blind ... a holiday from travel, and we talked, everyone to all. A guy I'd never seen – he told me how the country really was, what it had become ... the civil war, the comrades, the people shot and hidden, mounds; on the roadsides, or thrown in the streams, tossed down holes, disappeared into the sea....

'And when we started off again – I had been born. He made me militant, for all my life. It was my cause, to be defended to the limit, in every context and with anyone, to my disadvantage, never to my gain – crude and passionate – to no avail, none visible, a service, offering; to vindicate the missing ... to bear, to tell, the truth, Farjon. I was shown the sides, what they do and what they suffer, and I took my side, my allegiance, and I never left it, though....'

'It was impossible,' Bindi puts in, 'To be consistent. Because of contradictions. But you did it....'

'It turned out, that was the chance,' I say, 'To have me find a father: – a person with a treasure he could leave me ... a certainty....

'Still, it was truth I wanted, justice – not a family tree. And no contradictions came into it – just people. They make everything difficult. Unity ...The lizards grasp that. Humans don't.'

Farjon is too far ahead to hear, and Bindi is exhausted.

'Do we go down,' I ask, 'Into the fire? "The chamber", it is called.'

The climb is difficult. Either we don't speak, or I tell my story and nobody can hear. It often goes like that, and everything, it seems, is changed – usually the train runs perfectly, there are double tracks all over, and no one on the train takes time to speak to you.

You never see your father ever, never one more time. You don't know what language you each spoke, don't remember how he looked, if he was black or white, if he was your mother – it's not relevant.

'YOU LAUGH,

Bindi,' I say: 'It's good, it's healthy. But – that way you make yourself a creature negligible. You think laughing at us makes proportion, cuts us down. What if you're right?

'There's Farjon – look! He's entering the chamber, the cauldron. Maybe he read a paper that says – "any normal well-trained person can survive, just take the vaccine, and the sulphur and the heat won't hurt". Maybe it's true. But that, like all the rest – it isn't funny, not a bit.

'Farjon can claim sovereignty over anything – the explosions, the volcano – but not the house. Who knows where it might stop, his claim?'

'Oh,' says Bindi, much disconcerted, 'You only care about your house....'

'Industry, technology – for centuries it's been destroying, suffocating us, and now it's Farjon – trying to be a different kind of human, proof against the fire ...' I say.

'He's studied,' Bindi says, 'Those newts. You know what, Piet? – "those salamanders live in fire" – that's what they say. But – salamanders fake it. It's a tale.

'Farjon trained – he supports the flames for real.'

'I don't believe it, Bindi,' I tell her, amazed, 'But I don't believe so many things, one more it scarcely makes a difference now.'

'What are *you* trained for, Piet?' she asks: 'I must admit – it's my great deficiency. I am not trained, and do not fake. One day – I'll be valued for it, but right now – it means I'm not among the fit, not selected, not admired, and not among the ready ones. I follow tastes – it's quite irrelevant. It only means I must be flexible.

'I follow – I'm not strong, I don't persist, and don't insist, I don't have records that I've set or broke – my physique is nearly zero, like it's always been. I'll only live a century, enjoy myself for much much less ... I'll be admired for being feisty, but for decades – I shall be old: old hat.'

She laughs, looks to me for sympathy, or some complicity.

I say, 'The trained ones – are they so far ahead? They don't have tastes, they kill their wishes and delights: – they've only figures they must beat. They are endangered, or uncomfortable at least, for many many years – and then – pouf! ... they're dead or twisted out of shape....'

'That's not the point,' she says: 'They can resist, they're concentrated. They compete – they're wrestling with themselves, they don't need guys to push them, puff them up....'

'Intellect, resistance,' I begin: 'Concentration. Style – maybe that comes in – it's all quite different from what I'd thought....'

'They're stiff, we're ductile,' Bindi says, with regret. 'As for myself, my own soft power –I'll need a message which attracts the followers – millions, hundreds of millions that switch me on to hear my latest thought.

'Meanwhile – the strong ones tread the path that takes them to the cauldron, the limit, beyond what humans can support. And there ahead of everyone, is Farjon, the paragon – sovereign of the heights ... trained by himself to be the best; a higher, better level of mankind....'

'I must admit,' I say, 'I don't know what it's for: still less, what I might have done to beat him or be the second best. I understand that Farjon wants my house, the strongest house to hold him, where he's sovereign ... and yet, and yet ... It all seems modest. Trivial. A stunt, a sideshow.

'As though Houdini really broke steel chains...!'

We wait. The volcano hisses. Eventually, Farjon steps out, out of the cauldron. He is browned, there's a fine scent of – roast. Turkey? No – of crispy pork.

He seems unharmed. The first one of the tribe, the new one, that supports the flames? His brown hair – maybe a darker shade. That's it, except 'Your beard!' shouts Bindi. It is true – it's gone. The face – a Humpty-Dumpty brown: ... a 'before' the fall. Poor Humpty. There is not a crack. Not yet.

'Well done,' I say: 'Very well done indeed.'

There's nothing more to say. We take a snap to show he's fine: he holds some gadget that records the temperatures, and identifies the plants. He seems to be – the top.

The sovereignty? To show he's first? It's done this way: – with no flag, but personality ... the risk is thereby justified – the volcano could be his....

'No,' he says: 'It's just a trick. Volcanoes can't belong to anyone – my record is the heat endured, my title,' and we are much impressed, or so we say.

'Now,' I say, 'We go down the far side, and see what's what. Another plain, maybe a lake – red white or blue, with iron and cobalt, maybe silver too, lizards erect, constructing bowers – mandrakes, perhaps, with gloomy songs; and larks ascending – their coloratura invoking resurrection, insurrection too....'

There's silence. Farjon no doubt feels I have belittled him, his enterprise.

'I'm serious,' I say: 'Farjon has survived a wondrous test. It won't get him my house, but all the same – respect is due....'

We start the descent, my two guests in angry silence, Farjon limping, drags his bare burned feet....

'Was this,' I ask myself, 'Adventure? Or a sleight of body, an illusion? A true feat, significant perhaps, but arcane too: sacrifice of an immortal soul, sold for the devil's offer of supreme prowess. Then, uniqueness filed and forgotten in the archives?.... Records? Just stop-watches and streams of sweat....'

The ground before us smokes and shifts ... the greasy mist makes us light-headed, even euphoric. We feel we're guardians of our time, if not of space. The strangeness of the landscape – the changing roles with animals whose intelligence has overcome their incommunicability ... our movement up and down the boiling pyre – dreamlike, mythic, the original route-march. Out of Africa ...

Away, away from my poor brownstone sanctuary, the stagnation, the poor bombed, decaying houses, the roads ploughed up, the poles starting to sprout with yellow shoots, the gardens ruined, twiggy, as soiled as nests for storks. The mountain – it sets us up, lends visions, challenges....

It wins, defeats us. We can't see, nor hear. We turn around, go back. The record now belongs to Farjon.

The potential despot – still Bindi, in contention.

In short – nothing accomplished, except Farjon's trick.

The house, the ruined house, is safe for now ...

We retreat, demoralised.

I'm not unhappy, though.

*

'There's others like us on the way,' says Bindi: 'Better prepared, and less indulgent ... Poor Piet. With no resource but his long history of playing losing hands....'

'Remember, Bindi,' I'm angry, tell her: 'I don't always tell the truth. If anybody did, it would be overpowering.

'In music, you can show your strength – you're often on your own, there's no one there to trip you up, and in any case you can't fall down. I'm strong, when there's the need; stronger than the house, although the house is also me, but if it falls – I'll still be there....'

'It's empty,' Bindi says, 'Your ranting on. Like strength and shimmer in a music: – strength, integrity – those are tools: it's the language that composers have, so if you don't speak it you wouldn't understand....

'You are not strong, Piet – you just inherited a cause. You speak its language still.

'Farjon – was strong. He set the record ... now, he won't survive. That doesn't matter – surely, not to him.'

There's always sound, unfocussed. 'It's the waves,' I say: 'Yes, in the end, everything is swept away. The waves – they bring the wreckage back. Not people, naturally. They say the best are always with us – it isn't true. No one is, no one ever....

'Farjon has no aim to set a course. He's desperate, his power comes and goes, he has obsessions that he picks up here and there. His plan is just to leave us all behind. The Plan? A nothing, a hope, a lie.'

Piecing things together – fragments or contradictions, most mismatched. Why do things happen and not the things you want, people living side by side, who could cooperate, and don't, who prefer a nightmare – many, most of them, then all of them, when the war, the bombing and the expulsions start. Why does it surprise? Solidarity? The species – fighting to persist ... prefers an internecine battle.

Was mine a waste of time, a great, a stupid, impossibility? The struggle? Is it true, it nought avails?

Comrades. I trained them, sent them off, and often mourned them.

If the universe had an alternative, two destinies, if believers had two Gods – I'd be the left hand one, the commie, radical – the great persuader. I wouldn't ask for love ... only belief.

It's not turned out so: – a single God came top, one destiny: – adoration and conservatism, family, tradition; rescue the lost sheep, abolish purgatory, don't mention Hell, going strong as ever. Even stronger?

Monotheism – it seems a con, when there's alternative destinies, the lizards starting off again ... the giant birds rising – training to fly once more. Bigger, better. Evolution implies a pandemonium, a pantheon, the smaller deities thrust aside and dying out – fossilised, polished, ending on the shelf. One God – how the creators, ancestors – how they loved despotism!

Watch out for the self-styled Good Guy – divine patriot and family man, judge, saviour: genocides a speciality, creator of free will and evil deeds. Innocents abandoned, guilty set on thrones....

Myself? No, I don't belong in that company – unlike us, the Gods don't do campaigns, don't stand for justice. You worship them – that's it. The rest is up to you, until – there's re-birth or a pair of wings, or hell-fire for the rest of time.

Rights for anyone except themselves would break the rule, the privilege.

My! – but I need that place to live, the tall stone house, the cellar with the broken Sèvres, the celadons, chipped *famille rose* ... Everybody needs a stash. Some glue, and lots of time, and then the auction; clumsy repairs hidden, overlooked.

'Farjon thinks the house is symbolic,' I tell Bindi: 'It's nothing. It's all me....'

'Of course,' she says, patting my hand: 'Everything is you. Your crimes, your goodnesses – if there were ... all is symbol, if you want.'

'To listen to you, Bindi, it seems I'm paranoid,' I say, and laugh. 'I should confess – for what?'

'No, Piet, you aren't a victim, but you're old,' she says. 'It happens so: – no one remembers anything of you, your time, your friends. Time, preferably remembered and restored, and friends – the great romancers made a story out of these. Too bad, if you had only routine time, and dodgy boring friends. People will make up stories, sometimes you're the hero, often not,' she says. 'You, my dear, you are a "not". Humanity? All changed, all different, all angry, all now speaking English but, in reality – all different, uncomprehending, and quite indifferent to you: – your calls for peace and liberty, and for resistance, combat – it's all gone.... Forgotten, even, probably, by you ... The people who were sent all over, with your inspiration and your mission, so you say.... imaginary: or a depraved gang – spies and good-timers, every one....'

'Oh,' I say, dismayed, 'I believe you, naturally, except ... the lizards. Not my fault, nor my responsibility, not at all....'

She laughs. 'The house,' she says, 'It could be taken down, each stone dispersed – they'll make the milestones for a long long road....'

'You're a legend, Piet,' Farjon joins in, barely audible: 'You, your house still here – and all the rest destroyed. And yet the people you'd inspired – comrades, you call them: they didn't go. Or, if they went, not to anywhere you'd thought. That's why everything turned out different.'

'It's *really* different,' Bindi says: 'Especially now. It always was.'

'So? Go with the flow? Roll with the punch?' I ask. 'I don't believe in resolving problems, in understanding, nor in coexistence – I'd be crazy if I did.'

'You never know,' says Bindi, 'Whether you're useless, if you're betrayed, or if you're on the list. You live your years not knowing, sometimes – you suspect, because it isn't subtle, the fingering; nor meant to be. But it's as if, yes, you are a real human, living, dying. And all the time, behind you, there is somebody, a legion, who really knows; who writes your story, and the script determining what happens to you, and so you think you are betrayed when instead the word is being passed ... that you are not reliable. A spy, a traitor. Or, you may think you're useless when, instead, the word goes round – you're under an investigation, although probably, for reasons geopolitical or trivial, no case will come to court because you are exposed and powerless and besides – best not to let the secrets of the secrets out. Even – you might be framed....

'You might be smart, and blame the list ... you could be wrong. The list is like the sea – full of drowned sailors – and, on top – of pleasure boats....

'It's puzzling, because how things happen, why they do – intrigues you, but there's never in your grasp the real, banal, reason for what happens; that other people oversee and run your life – push you this way, and that. It's not a metaphor, a fear – it's real. It happens to an infinity of people, or to no one, nobody at all....'

'And, Bindi,' I ask, 'How come you know?'

'Oh,' she says, 'I worked on lists. My second job.

'I'm sure – there was some guilt around. I'm justified, I'm clean. You, Piet – you'd be accounted guilty as you're charged. That doesn't matter – you had radical thoughts and deeds; so what? – what matters is that what you made to happen, what happened back to you. Life was made to matter to you. Not by you. You too had your list, your hope to create lives – and all the time, we fingered you.

'For you – an inconvenience that spoiled your life.

'For others on the list – they met with nasty deaths. You are a lucky guy....'

'And this is an apology?' I ask.

'No,' she says: 'You took your stance. You should have taken seriously that you were spied upon, manipulated. Free will – that was your belief, your downfall. And besides – you were quite free – except, you were the rat in the psychologist's maze. Someone was placing barriers, and removing them, as you ran around. Testing and planning as you panicked. You lived in a rat-box, Piet – but you were free to be ingenious, persistent....'

'You gave it up, the work ... ?' I ask.

'They fired me. I was idle,' Bindi says: 'But I knew how to lead the sheep. That's what I want to be. Bellwether. So far – it hasn't worked. There's Farjon up ahead of me, drawing the crowds. But – no cash. He's cooked....'

'How simple! I might have suspected ... the lists ...' I say: 'My life was them, not me ...'.

I'll discount it ... ignore all this.

There was the bombing to explain, no list accounts for that....

And, I still occupy the house ...

'Are you sure about the bombs?' asks Farjon: 'Maybe your neighbours kept explosives, and got careless. There's gangs too, rife; tooled up heavy, eager....'

'People are envious of you, Piet,' Bindi says, 'You have civilisation, and you boast about it. You float above, on high.'

'Did they order you to train people, ship them off?' asks Farjon.

'Of course not,' I say: 'I obey no orders. I deal in universals. I educated – off they sailed, like weevils on ships' biscuits, nibbling at the colonial world, the despotisms ... as you know. You were a dilapidated part of that.... remittance men and women, to be blunt

... part of the baggage train, the would-be-goods who move in when they think the battle's done....

'I think of my guys, my pioneers, as missionaries, not conquistadors. Resistance? It's all conversion – if you suspect it's sleight of hand or tongue, you underestimate the power of faith, belief ... commitment to a change of course, of history, of culture ... useless to explain and analyse the consequences, the metamorphoses ... for those, there can't be blame, nor a congratulation....'

These two may be cops – the kind with more power and fewer checks. No uniforms outside, but inside themselves, forever on parade.

'We should all be cops,' says Farjon, 'You too, Piet. If you think there's laws sustaining the society you believe in, and you want to see them enforced ... then you're a cop.'

'And if not,' I say: 'Then I'm on the other side. Against the law. So, you could take me in and jail me. To make things clear, I'd need to make a declaration, a sort of confession. And yet – it isn't about law. It's judgement – I'd say "the judgement of me myself", only ... there's you two here ... Anyone can take a shot....'

'We could still take you in,' says Bindi, 'Not because "we judge it so", but to be sure you could be truly judged. You can be judged because you failed.'

'The wars are heavy now,' I say, 'Just like before. The ideologies are "lite", except – I'm not convinced ...those guys, the chiefs, they smell the same, prevaricate and bluster, set up battle lines, erase them, deepen them with sabre cuts ... just like before. They creep where once they strode. They're ready for the end of life, all life; and some of us are not....

'"Take me in" – that's a fine phrase! "In to jail...", or court – a law-court, not the "Sissi" kind....

'I'm stripped of everything I had, except what I have said. That, in some way, persists: is "me". My armour – is words now dissipating, becoming an abstraction. Though, I still have some concrete, to keep them in....'

'Yes,' Farjon says: 'Of course, the house. Your fine stone house. That is at stake....'

'Bombing and gangs,' I say – 'You can't resist, and yet – of course you can. There is no choice ... I'm not a victim – I'm a suspect. And I fought, resisted ... though I shan't tell you how.

'The destruction here? These events are horrible, the causes trivial or infantile. That's how we humans are, and why we won't prevail, persist.

'The alternative to me, of course, is, was, worse, much worse ... I've nothing to regret....

'I have my doubts about the robots – if they have our brains. They'll end up as we shall, and in quicker time....'

Terrible! All terrible! Everybody knows – not worth repeating ... Are we all part of this? Of course, and is that why we pass it over, silently – and talk about the house, volcano, Sonia's sweater ...? Yes, of course.

Leave it there.

'The floors aren't structural,' says Farjon, swarming along a beam. 'They just hang on the walls – so, it's all sound. The house will last another thousand years....'

'I'm sure, if it falls down,' I say, 'It'll show all has been a metaphor. We'll appear as figments, blown away like mist, and true immortals will collect remains... of us toys, the leg-shafts of painted lead, the hussars' caps, the leather cataphracts – and real life, somewhere, will go on – surely, no one will build successors to humanity, machines with super brains.... What folly! To use *our* brains as models ... Patience! Let's not go mad.'

'No!' says Bindi, 'You know: – we're all here today, and gone tomorrow. There is no other fate, no universal change. You want to see it different – but it's all the same. We depend on that: it is "reality".

'Now, Piet – see the new faces, fresh people plodding through the flood....'

'And will they capture me, and condemn ...' I ask.

'What you ranted on about – life conditions, and philosophy – the slogans on the coins – "equality!" Surely you recognised this meant revolution – the prams careering down the steps, the cossacks' horses lapping from Bernini fountains ... manifestos, decapitations ... what you wanted, irreversible. Uncertainty.

'That was not a simple line you crossed. You called for an upsetting of the real, of our historic referents: against our very nature. And for that, what did you think would be the punishment?' asks Bindi ... 'Hopeless! You wanted change, to change our history, and with that – everyone. And everything.'

CHLOE AND MAXIM

Chloe – she wades up to me, Maxim in her wake. Thirty-three, no family, Maxim looks the same age, a warrior? A graduate of communes now collapsed. Read books by people you've not heard of. Both Americans, and refugees. They know me? Want something from me – not the house, I hope.

To be mistrusted? Welcomed – who ever now can tell?

'Piet!' cries Chloe, 'Who was it invented reason? And you forgot? Why don't you use it?'

'Mathematics,' Maxim adds: 'It's universal – you don't require humans being good or bad, whatever their conditions, and their aims. It's like reason: – whatever universal may be right and true, it doesn't depend on humans who interpret, calculate. Whether you change the humans, or leave them as they are – reason, mathematics, science, they are independent of us, of the species as a whole, as it's been created and evolved and taught.... Whether we exist or not, what we've discovered is more right and lasting – eternal – than we shall ever be. It was there already, waiting.

Who set it up? Maybe wind air and dust – just take those forms. We, all humans, whether we roast or freeze, drown or fly, are or are not: – the universals won't be wrong. They'll be forever independent of us, and indifferent ... deities of emptiness....'

'You mean,' I say, 'You can do to me, to anyone, whatever you might want – and reason is indifferent?'

They confer: 'It doesn't count,' says Maxim finally: 'It is another ... universe. Another neck – of the forest and the woods. Pure reason doesn't enter in for us, nor you. Your nature owes nothing to a reason you might invoke, except – maybe – you have the urge to live and kill. *That* reasoning is "Kant's irony".'

'So,' I say, 'Reason gives tools, procedures – nothing more; but stays forever without impact, from you and all the other beasts? We live life without Reason, without a justification, guide: only self-interested calculation ... Reason is true – we ignore it, and all other universals, as we wish....'

'I can throw down your house,' says Chloe, 'Without Reason, and without a justification. And – I could feel a-minded so to do, if a shelter's what I want. Or stones. That's my reason. And boo to your dismay ... attachment to possessions – ha-ha!'

'Let's step back,' I say: 'I know – my life has been one of fraud and skulduggery – not what I sought: – I was the running rat ... But think! By reason: – do you mean the slippery brain? Or spiky logic? Or survival – knowing the limitations ... Not exactly reason ... and besides the brain, who is a stranger who we never see but makes us walk and breathe – there's language. Still more slippery. Or maybe – the brain's the pot, and language is spaghetti, coiled like a gorgon's serpents in his hair ... Imagine: the water and the bombs: and now expropriation.

'The water rising – resulting from our wish to self-destruct, ignore the warnings, doing exactly what we and our many bosses wanted ... The bombs – for fear of our resistance and our faiths: – all our potential, down like the rain.... All are punished. Aggressors, same as us, the victims. We suffered for our evident humanity, a punishment followed, swift. Our life, our humanity, rampant, was unacceptable for its vivacity, and for its ordinariness.

'And now – the fine stone house – where my civilisation lives. Small, much reduced, decrepit – but ... still talking, still grinding out the tunes....'

'This isn't it at all,' says Maxim: 'You, Piet, are emblematic – small, closed like a penknife, browned and beetle-browed. Like your lookalikes, your fellows. Not appetising, not at all. A person who might employ people who would break our legs. Seduce. Drug our kids, then shoot them ... Can we trust you now, when you are senile, thinking of inventing memoirs?'

'Oh,' I say, 'Most groups are unappetising. The way we argue! I'm one of those – once I had certainty. Now, I criticise those who think they have....

'Faith – it interests me. Faith in religion? In what happens? In what you yourself can do? Religions – the rites, recognising people like you ... and the unlike, condemned for all eternity ... Your co-religionists, sharing a mystery, an ignorance, something archaic, polished up.... what bores!'

'I'm for Bindi,' Chloe says: 'She invites abuse, playing the waiting game, alas. She's vulnerable to any fisher with a line – even old Piet....'

'They never mentioned it to me,' I say: 'Not her ingenuousness. Not religion. The neighbours who were creamed, what did they believe? Faith? To me, it's a dead thing. I was devoted to explore the mystery. A detective's work – that leads to condemnations....'

That was unpopular. Maybe people like a plot, a fraud you can trust, believe in. A loyalty to something that's invisible ... not shared. A treachery, because you can't admit, those faiths – it's all hypothesis. It's an hypothesis that you enjoy: – being forever at the start and favoured, when others are already sparring with the end, the Death.

'You can't claim the house,' says Chloe: 'It isn't yours, you have no title.'

'Of course I don't,' I say: 'I don't believe in property, possession of property ... besides, it's a place to live, and after death – there is no property. The house is damaged, not enjoyable – part of my life that's crumbling down.'

'That isn't relevant,' says Maxim: 'Property passes down the chain – forever. Now – remember, there are many desperate, and they need your space.'

'It won't ever be the same,' I say: 'It will be spoiled, more spoiled, destroyed absolutely if you throw me out.'

Chloe and Maxim laugh.

'There's nothing happening here,' says Maxim: 'Just an oldster, keeping valuable people in the wet.'

'They all think their civilisation was the only, and the best,' says Chloe: 'Ignore him ... love him if you can.'

'I think you're right,' I say: 'About my civilisation, as it's called. That's not my point – although I know, I'm a failure, and always, I am wrong.'

'We've tried to stand you up, old guy,' says Maxim, 'But you – you just slump down again. You ought to leave – the house is shot, they'll hound you till you're dead ... the good clean guys; they'll put you on another list. You need to see that your adventure's dead. The old stone house – is crumbling, empty, except for the relics, the broken blundered pieces that will reproduce until they can't – like Teotihuacan I, degrading down through to Teotihuacan V. As civilisation swells, it uglifies, each of its epochs, down to the end....

'You see the cycle, Piet, but you don't see what it's like, to live in one that's dying: dead. You think "Oh, it'll be off again – a different style, discoveries anew, a fresh new pair of Gods and human sacrifices done with taste." No, you're in the crash! All you have, inside and out – becomes a burden, obsolete at once –

the language, clothes, courtship – just to start.... the flower vase and the pet – all changed.

'That's how it happens, my old friend – the civilisation's over, and you won't gain admittance to any other one. Barbarians will take you – if you're lucky. Most likely a Dark Age until you've croaked.

'It's finished, Piet! These civilisations, call them cultures, even – they go on spawning copies, like a machine – but watch it! The photocopiers will catch your coat and drag you in – under the light, the rollers ... and then you're done. Along with all the other corpses they have made.... you're copied! A clone, a simulacrum, ghost!'

'The volcano!' Bindi shouts, and interrupts: 'We'll all go up again, and take poor Piet as well. As for his abusing me – he's an old scarecrow, quite incapable, as you see....'

THE OILY TREES

The old house – yes, it's empty, evidently very old. I lay poor Farjon on a raft, a floating catafalque – in the flooded library, still with shelving but no books. He's no longer hot: he's very cold. His shell, his face – is bluey-green – ah! I think – if only, when we die we could be born again, from blue-green eggs; as blackbirds. Aggressive, just like us, but creative, master-singers quite unlike you and I, who need a training, years of slog and then – quite shaky, amateur ... Farjon, though, now holds the record. He's satisfied ... a failure too, not capturing the house....

The house – a shell: – look up, it's hollow as a lift-shaft, a cathedral, an office block. Of course it isn't mine – it's rocks ... You see the lizards crouched, sculpted within the walls, the little raptors fossilised – komodo dragons too, ensconced in the old stones. There's no hint of us, the human squatters, leaving their rubbish as they left the site: no bone, no epigraph. It's good.

Mine goes where all the civilisations go – under the trees, the soil, the lakes ... just leave them there, and read a book, a palm: be informed, don't marvel, don't bring your spades.

As for Farjon – he won't tell you anything, not anything at all.

All four of us – up to the mountain. Farjon – champion, moribund, left for dead.

Bindi – happy for Farjon, sad for herself, and, when she can reflect – sad for him as well ... Me? I keep my sadness for myself.

Onward and upward – futility of conquest, but – climb to the top and plant the flag. And – I'm in the game. True, it's the civilisation's theme, it's how the powerful reproduce themselves, abase the rest – but ... I've been a failure, as I've said. Forced enjoyment, as it's called, climbing the peaks: – like going to a museum, a gallery, a concert-hall ... I'd rather listen to the frog chorus from the wetlands, the cicadas ... out of our range, out of our tutelage; by our and their good luck....

*

The corn, the lizards – they have gone. Lizards – did we think they'd magnify, burst their bounds – swell, again becoming maxi dinos in the rocks, the sand ... did we expect them to do well – to grow and scheme? Too bad! They've disappeared. Could they be thrusting somewhere else? ... or body-building, sub-species multiplied, in vain?

Do you only have one go, the one enormity of years, the single spin? Then, starting small again? And staying so; despite the gym, the elocution? Flying, roaring – no earthly use at all ... Taking your chance, your luck, too late ... You've had your time! Your age has gone – resign yourselves to being small and fleeting ... Think on that, mankind! Enjoy your turn, don't seek another one....

There's green and oily trees instead – we have to force our way ... Maxim's machete – useless, you would need an axe.

THE FIRE

On we go, and on and on. We can't see higher, it's all oily trees.

'I'm sure the grease is good,' says Bindi: 'Put in cakes, or on your face – or even on your bicycle....'

And she smears all over – purple, blue, and red.

There is a groaning rumble – and we're sprayed. Down comes a burning smelly mist ... No need to point out: we're a wormy crew – the aeroplane poisons us, flies off....

'It's good,' says Maxim, making a Santa face and, using both his thumbs, he stuffs his mouth with gloop the aeroplane has dropped. 'Try it, everybody!', he insists, although we won't: 'More poison! It's become our nourishment – enjoy!'.

Bindi laments, 'Oh no! My face is forever set and streaked,' and so it is ... the pesticide a *vernissage*.

'It's civilisation and identity,' I say –'Design indelible, the colours too. In one swoop, poor Bindi, you've been identified. Maybe wrong on all accounts, but bear with it. Imitating the first societies – it's fashionable ...painted and doomed.'

But Bindi can't be reconciled – she scrubs her face until there is a stippling of scarlet pustules in the streaks – 'And where's the mountain gone?' I ask.

Fire – everywhere.

Fire and water – sweep everything away.

There comes a clearing on the plain – there's not a bird, a goat or anything alive but us. The mountain's gone, quite flat – a boil that's lanced, the pus distributed, but you can see inside, the fire that burns beneath us all – it's seething red. I peer right down – there's Farjon's sneakers abandoned on a rock – the 'Victory' trademark still quite plain ...and in the roaring fire you see the shapes, the tumbling and the writhing flames, and molten stone.

'It's where the abstract and the concrete form,' I say: 'Still inchoate: as one, still indissoluble – but when the magma is expelled, abstract and concrete will divide, and philosophers, for all the human species' time, its lease on life – will try to stick them back together, re-join the concrete and the abstract – in harmony or tandem, overlaid ... to re-compose a unity. Restore the Revelation, in a word.

'It's what the monks, the lamas, all blowing trumpets –the *bodhisattvas*, the dead illuminated – the *tantrikas* pressing cheek to jowl – all aim at, aspire to ... But, wait! The fire.

'It underlies us all, its power ... Death, puny in comparison, and weak. Not friendly, though.

'Philosophy defeated by the fiery furnace, as it was written long ago. We see the formation of our thought – its imperfection, fancy footings, soft-shoe shuffling – how it impresses: but, alas, does not illuminate.'

Doubts assail me – it is true, that abstract, concrete, are both fluid, bubbling: – both seem concrete, and yet, as the shapes dissolve, re-form – you'd say that both were abstract too. Or concrete after all and always all too concrete, as poor Farjon found.

I'm confused, out of my depth.

All my causes, all these countries, peoples – finishing in sink-holes – soon, quite soon – or wandering over new uncharted deserts, somewhere, somewhere else. All that is concrete – ends in abstraction, in history – or just disappears.... new, very ancient, peoples, ideas – up they come, like islands rising from the sea ...

And can it be, that all that boils – is language? A sport, a flick of tongue? A trick, a prowess, as the talking lizard tried? Not invention or technique, or industry: not sentiment, and not intelligence: – just talk: some casual – what comes to mind; some pondered, some from Dante settling scores in hell, and some from

God and some from Proust, those well-heeled friends ... After all, this is the field where concrete and abstract – when they are made to float, transcend – they levitate, turn into our daily communication, daily baguette, and common referents....

'The mountain, volcano, Piet?' Chloe interrogates, dismayed – 'Can it be so – it slid away and leaves this wound exposed ... the engine of the world? Oven? Incinerator? Throbs, glows beneath our soles....'

'Time,' I say: 'We wanted to accelerate our time – to have it run away from us and speed a cure for everything: even, rush in successors, brainier types ... or else a gadget that would sweep our disadvantages away, and soothe the turbulence....'

Far off – we see a streak, a black horizon – a stony beach of lava, and beyond – the Sea! The mountain must have melted, flowed down to the beach....

'It has all changed!' I say: 'Look! Bindi has found a civilisation on her face, Farjon is dead, perhaps still fertile, and could transform, become a blackbird – if he has the luck....

'And now look back! The old stone house looks newly targeted and skewed – maybe a reprisal, drone, or maybe subsidence....'

Chloe and Maxim – they don't grasp my thought. 'There!' they shout, 'Look over there! What should we do...? Forget the trees ... the Sea, the Sea!'

'Strip off,' shouts Bindi, 'Let the prickly waves break in my face, and maybe I shall lose my streaks....'

And down we run, tearing off our clothes, rejuvenated and without a clue, down to the water, over the cool black slab of rock... into the scalding waves....

I try to reflect, and pause: my principles? Freedom and justice – or a swim? The scales of justice jigger up and down, the Statue's bandage drops from her blinded eyes.... I give thanks there's no reprisal, provocation – no bombardment ... In we plunge – we roll like seals or sea-lions, bark like otters....

This is the crux. Perhaps.

We frolic in the boisterous waves – our distressed bodies change their shapes – breasts sprout, the penises recede, the body hair is sloughed, becomes a seaweed tangle on the shore, our ears are mussels in their shells, the embarrassed octopus backs delicately, fits snug into our mouth – her cave....

Our navels spout, creating pools where life – real life! – wriggles and gulps, intestinal flora protect the miniature beasts: – their enormous mouths a-gape, their tiny eyes glint like the jewels in grandpa's watch.

We're one with nature. It's exhausting, it turns us inside out – our hearts beat slow, slow as the waves, our blood – 'blue as the sea,' says Maxim, belly-boarding, borne right up the rocky beach.

We lie, side by side, doze on the volcanic spew, the black discharge.

The sea was scalding hot. Fish – will be broiled, like us. We have baked skins, like well-cooked spuds – a brown black pink.

'...Time once again to show off, Piet,' I think. 'Show them you have an analytic power ... Beware, I'm full of ploys and tricks. Ah! Maxim,' I shake him full awake, a-brim with urgency: 'Let me explain myself ... my secret dread ... someone might take away my house, before I'm done with it.'

He's now a friend. Our congress with the sea, the beach, has made us twins – we're *semblables*, blood brothers in the skin, the shell. Hot water softens you, makes you more malleable – but still, I'm far beyond a physical bond of any kind with him, no twitch, no sexual interest ... in anyone, myself as well....

'The old stone house,' I say: 'It is my home, you know. Like crabs who nest in empty cans....'

'Oh,' Maxim says, 'It's quite collapsed. We wanted to see in, to study it, no more.... While being harried round the States, I tried, rejected, many strategies: – communes, secession, starting again – all to make a civilised place, like you once had....'

'Or I have still,' I put in. 'I sought a terrain where our old civilisation had long since beached. A settlement surviving on the edge. Stranded. I hoped to find somewhere that I could change, revive, in its last gasp....'

'Revolution – you've been through that,' he says: 'It's language; so, at least, you've been reduced to say. In reality – it would be much more difficult than you're prepared to face. You wouldn't live it through ...

'Reforms? Your neighbours left their houses when there wasn't work for them to do, cash to earn – so, what reforms? You never let them in the fine stone house, besides, they didn't want to come – and now, it's ruined, uninhabitable. Our civil war....'

'I've always been in civil wars,' I interrupt.

'They made it definite this time,' he says: 'Where we were. The best hope for you, for anyone – was jail for all eternity: death row, or the marines. There'd be no chance for the house....'

'Oh,' I say, dismayed: 'I can show folk round.... It's hugely tall, and empty as the sky....'

'There's nothing left to see but bits of what there was, and people gluing shards,' he says: 'For sure, the more some stuff resembles what there once had been, the more it's a success. But recognise it, Piet – you have survived, but you have failed in every other way....'

'That's worse, Maxim,' I say, as we cool down, our bodies bloat back to how they were before the sea transmogrified us, 'Than if you want to steal my house.

'Failure for me? Processions of bosses, feeling good, living high on the hog, and then ... offset by more disasters for us all, that cannot be resolved. And wow! look how the crises multiply.... all the best people killed who might have known....'

'Civilisations,' Maxim says, 'They're not stolen – diffusion is their point. They spread, until they can't, and that is it! Then, they are buried, deserted when they've done. They live by what will bring them down.

'You wanted change, conversion, clarity. Too bad. Now, no one bothers with all that – they know they'll have an ugly death, quite soon. The weak, whole populations, they are killed, without a word, but lots of bangs. The stronger – they die slow– the water, fire, earth, and air – the elements will poison them ... they breathe, they sleep and drink and eat, they are consumed by living bad – no one enjoys carefree old age....

'The old stone house – you'll dynamite it, maybe? Anyway, it'll fall down ... and it's now a burial place – a first step to the past? A *kurgan*, a burial mound.... Not to be dug up, don't forget....'

We make the hand-sign, a *scongiuro,* for Farjon: remembering he's dead, laid out. And how we don't want to be.

We pause.

'Maxim, old friend,' I say, 'I should tell you – I'm in therapy for senility. The lady, Sonia, my figment – she's good! Sorted out abstract and concrete for me. When there's only abstract – you have won! They call it paradise!'

'I've been round the fine stone house,' Chloe says: 'You must be *her* figment – certainly, there's not much concrete left. No books, no photos, pictures....'

'Oh,' I say, 'All over the world, they read and see the same. That must be what you mean, when you say there's not much civilisation in the house. No furniture, no entertainment, and no art. No, there's no bric-à-brac....'

'Thinking of what's civilised, I mean – those people, killed, threatened, kept in, kept out; in prison, on the street,' she says, 'They're casualties of a civilisation, their own – although I know all that sounds trite. The civilised take excesses in their stride ... They squeaky-clean their principles so that no dirt sticks; like Bindi wants, as she tries to restore her face.'

'Chloe,' I say, 'You think that everybody might have your sensibility. Yet – it's clear, that's not a universal, not useful ... it's toxic, so, they limit sensibility. It's sense. Integrity? Perhaps turned into something else you didn't want, consensus, probably.'

'Piet has everything in his head,' says Maxim, laughing: 'You can't take anything away from him, nor add. Maybe he wishes scepticism and doubt was not in there, but I'll bet they are....'

'For sure they are,' I say: 'But let it be. Let's say there are no doubts, and no uncertainties. Let's say "I'm home". For me, no looking for a new stone house, no more neighbours who will have to move again because of me....'

'That isn't why they had to move,' says Chloe: 'It was all the rest you didn't have, and didn't bring – and don't know what it would have been.'

'It's too late now,' I say, 'And anyway – you two escaped from over there. That isn't an accomplishment. It was self-preservation, not a self-defence.'

'I know,' says Maxim, 'That was a mistake – like staying there would be. Mostly – you can't do anything at all that's right ... but, at least, I did enjoy the sea, despite the heat....'

'It's not enough,'says Chloe: 'Not for me – just to flee. I never ran away before this time, with him. I was much closer to the core: the faith, the mission – more than you were, Maxim – I was into the critique, and the hope I could regenerate the place. We must avoid an end like Piet's, is all. The most he did – was get put on a list ... We seek....'

She doesn't finish.

'Bindi shouldn't stay,' I say: 'If you leave soon, take her along. She needs protection. She has a plan, but one that needs some lies to make it plausible. It needs promotion, polish too.'

'Hey,' Maxim says, pressing on, 'At least – you'll need a memoir of us two. A picture? Portrait. Otherwise it seems the plot does not exist and the characters, us, aren't real.'

'All right,' I say: 'A snap will do.'

And there they are – Bindi in war-paint, clinging to Chloe, who wears smart black pants, a white frilled blouse – she fled straight from work – and at their feet lies Maxim, open-mouthed and panting like a sheep-dog, from the heat. All is decked, fore- and back-grounded, in white: as if the snow – the light – got in.

Then – they leave – but, before they left....

PARTING

'I was at Vassar,' Chloe says, 'In graduate school, they gave us this, in case we were ever in a spot, or one like we're in now. It's *plastique*....'

And so it is. She stuffs it into cracks, all round the walls. 'When you're convinced,' she says, 'the excess has gone too far, there's no way out, your time is up – the water's rising, and the heat is, too.... Just set it off – and you – you and the house – will make a massive *kurgan*.'

'Today was inspirational,' I say: 'Bear with me, a little while. I'm interested in what I am, have been, and where I find myself. I'll talk....'

Indeed – unstoppable. The talking cure. No cure, of course, but you find all about your therapist. Your audience.

'You need to put each point into a narrative,' says Chloe: 'It gives it shape, there is a pattern – the matrix will be you, and so ... it's clear. You ended so or so, and bad, because....'

'No,' Maxim says: 'The context must come first, then you introduce the subject: Piet. Without the context, he is indecipherable.'

The story ... my life ... quick, quick, compress it, while there is a moment ...!

'I analyse, blossom with rhetoric, and possibly someone – no, *someone* – trips me up each time,' I start, 'and every little fault or

greater one they see, is magnified, and weighted with
significance. Might I have succeeded, keeping quiet? I wouldn't
have heard a word of what I thought. Without the statements,
there's no accusation so no condemnation. It was never
understood, my wish to overturn, dismantle, harm, dismember
and expose – everything that was, existed ... everything set over
us. With or without my comrades, Party, fellow-travellers and
proletarians – foot-draggers, all – or nobody at all! And, add to
that the unconcern, stupidity, of those who toted, dug and guarded
– the wretched of the earth – who suffered and then harnessed up,
and drove the immense tumbrels that took....'

'The population to the scaffold,' Maxim finishes. 'And to the
battlefield. It's what I said – you didn't see the civilisation that
you wanted to transform was moribund, while still it waved its
weapons, shouted war cries....'

'And killed like it was reaping corn,' says Bindi. 'You, Piet,
valiant like Childe Roland! Sneaking away, and "to the Dark
Tower came...."'

And we laugh.

'A context with pizzazz would have silenced you, put you
down, away – dropped you from a 'plane into the sea,' says
Maxim. 'Where you went wrong – was to mistake the nature of
the habitat. You were confused in your idea of what your
civilisation was. You saw it close up, had come from it, and even
loved its quirks and chants – but did not recognise how near its
end it was, how unredeemable ... how few your allies really were,
how fickle and how ill-prepared.

That civilisation – it is finished; unmoving, dead. Nothing to
be achieved there, nothing at all.'

I take this in. Is it new insight? It would eliminate me....

'Your communes were hermetic, Maxim. Last chance saloons.
Not a shout was heard outside – they were a refuge, a retreat,' says
Chloe.

'We knew it,' Maxim says, 'They were exactly all they could have been. I – we – were correct. Piet could not have changed the context superficially, still less make the sea-change he'd proposed. The world made of potter's clay, the open, explorable world he thought he worked in, had long since petrified, pegged out. Strange death, but definite: the material, the future – had become granitic, and unworkable.'

'I couldn't win; agreed,' I say: 'It was just made harder by the interferences. I instructed, motivated – sent them out, the militants. All up to them? I wagered on the future, probably too much.

'And now, I'm sorted out, and thank you, Maxim, thank you Chloe. I'm not satisfied, but now, all can be accounted for....

The bombing? Over everywhere? Wars, effects of war. Isn't it all new? So extensive and unstoppable? The causes – throwbacks? The despots, the thefts, the territories that you say are yours – isn't it all different? or the same, archaic? More intense than before? Or similar – but repetitive, a crescendo ... More final? Irresolvable.

Maxim means this: – what we called civilisation: – flattened, expelled, exterminated. We fantasised, of course ... about the way we are....

It's time to mourn alone, I think.

'So, now – where will you go, my friends?' I ask, abstracted.

It's a terrible verdict I just heard. I need time, a length of time....

I go on, 'I see I failed because there was no chance of a success. But still – I have the stone house left. It's a ruin, but I must decide what's to be done with it: in it....'

'Oh,' Chloe says: 'It did you good to get all that fear and anger out. And us? Where to go? Everywhere is planned and mapped, we're visible like bugs that walk across a piece of pie ... We'll have to find a frontier somewhere, of some kind, cross it, find a place....' She stops.

'... a place to ...?' I prompt her, but she won't go on

*

The horses? I confess, I don't feel the same for lizards as I do for them....

And neither seems to have a place....

*

It's clear – I can't manage here, not on my own. Still, I'm an asset, not a burden, I can go with them, keep up....

'HEY!' I shout, 'You can't go off and leave me here!'

'Of course we can!' I hear a voice – Chloe's. Already far away, and moving right along....

'Finished,' I hear Maxim shout, 'Finished, done! When it's done, it's finished, Piet.'

The adventure's over? No new humanity, no enterprising novel gender, guaranteed and trouble-free, available to all; no resolution of the crises at our feet, over our heads. Nothing new, except for gadgets.

I'm stuck here. Abandoned.

The fine stone house – stands as a tower, a monument, until it falls – a mausoleum unattributed.

Certainly, it will not bear my name.

CAVING

'I associate you with that cinema person,' says Constantin: ' – a rising star, reserved, charismatic too, they say – who overdosed on heroin. He must have had a dark place – a desert, a forest ... they say that. And you, you're really dark. I'd love to know, to be let in, to share – like, I'm sure I have one too. A place you visit on your own. What did you bring back?'

'Nothing,' I say: 'Nothing at all. That's why they call it "dark". It could be "empty".'

I think – rooms are empty, but you can't just 'be' in an empty room – it's all joined on to 'somewhere'. That empty room you go to where you can't be reached – the point is not that it's empty, but it's not attached, not joined on to 'somewhere'.

Cinema? Stars? We're all on camera, all in rockets going up to where we came from: – stardust. It's a fantasy, and we live by it. Here and back again?

There's silence. He picks a piece of green: 'Thyme,' he says, rubbing a sprig: '"Time". People, even when they were apes – they did this gesture. It's as old as we are. When it gets too hot, it doesn't grow. That shows it wasn't hot, not so hot, when the monkeys started off....'

I know – how he pretends to be a stupid, to start a conversation off, so that later, he twists and bites, to show he's played with you, fooled you.

I'm not fooled, but it doesn't stop him, not at all.

Time – the monkeys saw it as a game. Time. Wait and pounce ... steal and cuddle. Play it, use it. Start it off – you can't stop it till you start. Stop when you get to the best bit – stop, if you can, if there is....

'It matters, Constantin,' I say: 'If we're not here. What was it for ...?'

'So, you're into mysticism. Religion,' he says.

'Neither – I want the truth. I've not got much time left, so it's now or never. It's personal,' I say: 'I want the truth.

'Suppose I'm shaman of the world. I want something lasting. Not fairy-tales, no improvisation. I want guys to sacrifice themselves for what I can invent, to show they have the faith. No "Spirit", no invisibles.'

That's what I mean by 'truth'.

We've all mostly been converted, and we don't lose it, the 'something', the ineffable mystery, even when we've betrayed, forgotten. But conversion to something you don't know, that may not exist, exist so you would recognise it, and know what a next step was ... that's problematic. Step from the void – you don't find land, a rock – just deeper voids.

Laboratories, white coats? Science. We all die, so we must all be sick. Fatalities from day one. There's lots of mystics, scores of religions – those must be causes, and not cures.

Or not relevant. Love, families – most people have a chance at those – they can be classed as therapies, but not as cures for anything.

You'd say 'death isn't relevant either. Don't take it so seriously, don't take it to heart ... the motor fuses – just for now, there's no repair, no spare. Too bad. Your destiny – to be born too soon, when there's ageing and dementia. No revelation, just confusion and fighting to get more air. More time.'

It may be so.

He says, 'You were sacked from teaching, for that approach, Socratic – 'I know nothing, but ask me something you don't know. I'll show off. I know everything.' Too sophisticated. To teach, you need have something that you know, or you pretend. You show a source: – you read it somewhere, and to prove what you say is true, some smart kid finds a source and ... there you are! It's guaranteed. The proof....'

We laugh.

He goes on, 'I was in the circus, until they threw all us animals out. The tamers – unemployed: the rest – sent to the butchers'.

'People have it upside down, and backward. They think it's humans showing how they can subdue the animals and have them do all kinds of silly tricks. It's the reverse. The animals – behind the scenes, they do us down. They kill us, the "trainers": mutilate, disfigure ... Ostriches – that big middle toe – straight in your diaphragm, like breaking through a paper screen; you couldn't breathe.... The wolf – took all the flesh from off your arm, it didn't hurt, but then he broke the bone, didn't gnaw or suck the marrow: but *that* hurt, and how! The lions are dozy, but the rhino gets you against a wall and leans on you – a trick the zebras have as well. Crushes your ribs and lungs. Those little pigs – sharp hooves, and trample on you, all over, snuffing you, snuffing you up....

'Look at me! All discoloured and twisted, bones exposed, see how green they grow. Complain to the management? Don't think of it.

'The punishment? The cold water down inside your pants....'

Both looking for a new job, and both find the perfect one. Perfect for our past, our skills. Everything we tried, couldn't do, and cheated at.

Spotting.

Journalists with field-glasses, watching for the start of world war three – or is it four? Our civilisation can't resolve ... not threats from the outside, not from within. That is the priority of civilisations – spot, manufacture, defend, against the threats. Not one can do it. They all fall. This one brings us all down with it.

The catastrophes it brought on itself – the trees cut down, the floods, the droughts, obesity and famine.... not to mention the democracy which doesn't work and lurches towards despotisms – those are threats too. The past – how it attracts, drags us back: can't get enough of them – dictators, wars and genocides.

No one can doubt them, despots: – they're not about territory or prestige or rights or challenges to profits, no: they burn you, drown you, infect you with the creeping pox.

From this high hill, we watch the mountains round about. All quiet, until we'll see a shape move up – a tank, a gun – or things we don't see, not at all – up higher, and then you never hear the bang – nor anything at all, not ever more.

'Tell me,' he says, 'I may have missed that day in journalism school. What is it, exactly, we are watching for, and when we see it – what does it signify?'

'If the two fronts, the two wars, join up by military action up high there – then, it's the next world war,' I say: 'The alliances – like in the first war – will pull each other in, form different sides. They are constrained to mobilise at different speeds, with different objectives, and enthusiasms ... but all will declare, prepare, for war, alert their populations ... win, lose, capitulate, pull out....'

'To prepare for death,' he adds.

'Yes,' I say: 'That is so, although it may be an exaggerated calculation at this stage.... You never know, not quite – there's usually survivors whatever massacre occurs, someone is overlooked, is sheltering, or out of place....'

'You know,' he says, 'All great happenings need a witness, we are spotters, that I know, but in the end, it's other guys who puff the news, inflate it, put it in proportion, scare the crowds, and coin the phrases. We, who spot and pass it on – we are forgotten. Much more to the point is making art – the song, the phrase. It's like the *narco-corrido* in Mexico – the power-song that celebrates the cartel boss, makes reputations – the leader, and the songster too. Sinaloa – that's the place. Let's make the show, and be immune.'

'That's nonsense,' I tell him: 'Those musicians are deep in the game. They join the war of influence between the leaders of cartels, or factions in them. They're so close to the scene that if they make false moves – they're killed. That's absolutely not for us....'

It's dangerous enough to do what we're supposed to do. We're spotters for the news, TV – but we could equally be spotters for artillery of one or other side: – enablers, you'd say.

I think, but do not say, my colleague has a gift for fantasy, surrealist imagination, like his spiel about the circus as a spectacle where the humans are tortured, mutilated, by the animals they're presumed to dominate and train ...

Don't the tamers have a chance? Must they be eaten up?

Who knows what chance there is? The tamer, naturally. Behind the tent, the caravans – the animals always win. We pay, we, the audience, to see the exception, where we humans are on top, and animals obey ... Chance? Another fraud.

'So,' I say, 'You left the circus to avoid the torment, the threat – those ostriches....'

He stares at me. 'It was my con, you idiot,' he says, 'A nonsense, set to pass the time. Because.... you idiot, it's metaphor. The bosses always win. We practise tumbling, behind the caravans. The big beasts – they gang up. Underfed. We're killed – but in the ring – we win. Silly frolics. Yahoo! Fright wig and top hat! Supreme humanity....'

It's clear. Both know – there's no hope a side will pull a tank, artillery piece, up to the mountain crest, give warning, fire an opening shot. We're there as sacrifices. When it's time, they'll fire a rocket from afar – our silence; death.

That is the proof the fronts have joined ... The local wars become the Big One we've been trained to fear ... and we're the smoking flesh that proves it all....

'Fear,' says Constantin, 'Is something always there – there's no defence, it grows and grows, there is no respite and no remedy.'

We wait. We don't need those binoculars.

Nothing.

'You realise,' he says, 'They might not waste a rocket on us two. Besides – we are the ones who give the news. True – if we're killed, that's quite definitive. 'The war has grown. The witnesses are dead.' But isn't it more likely they would leave us with the scoop – one side or other would begin hostilities, and we'd be left to tell the boss?'

'It could be so,' I say: 'But we don't get a name, nor fame, for being messengers. Or starting blocks.'

'It's so,' he says: 'But then, remember, you always need in store another plan, or maybe more: – alternatives. For instance – you and I could start a group ... rock or rap ... We're full of sentiment – enough, that if we turn our feelings into rhythmic landscapes – we'd have a modest presence, make a name, a "we were there"....'

We wait. There's no expectancy – we know what will happen. Or – it won't, but it's more likely that it will.

'It reminds me,' says Constantin, 'The cinema person, overdosing. There's so many on the team, to make a movie – and, yes, almost each one moves. Though you'd say – not every novel is novel, nor romance, romantic. The novelty – what does it owe to the squad behind the inspiration and the marketing? "What's new" – are novels full of novelty? Beware! It can't be done.

'The focus-puller – she has feelings, a life, a story, many, maybe – she might overdose ... And – who makes the movie move...?'

'I think you're coasting towards something quite different, and new,' I say. 'Time here – is shaping rocks? Time changes rocks, creates a fossil from the thoughtless casual lizard.

'The movies all last 90 minutes, or two hours, some even more ... but almost always – you know when it ends, and starts. Time will not have an end: – the movie – every time.

'With time, there's always something new – the novel? Maybe there's misnomer here. Novel implies novelty? Not so....

'The movies – they're about time. The time they need to fit their space ...' I say.

'You're wrong,' he says: 'Confused. It isn't time.'

He may be right.

'Time?' he says, 'It changes nothing, doesn't move or act. The same with books,' he says, thoughtfully: 'The pages. War and Peace goes long, and Proust and Musil even longer – but there is a central character – the reader, reading. Excluded, but essential – the Mover. You! ... Reading at a certain speed, like the projector. Time again? No, it's *you. You* make it move. It's your call. Fitting the story in. And *leaving nothing out*.... Making speed and sticking to it.'

And he snarls the last words.

'I know,' I say: 'Is it just mechanical? Life goes slow and quick – the book cannot, it is confined in its own space, in how you turn the page – maybe you're slow – but what you get is just the same as anyone, like a portion in a restaurant....

'I heard, it's true, that space and time are the same thing, or not a thing or things at all.

'Refresh me, Constantin. What is speed? Is it true that something that doesn't move at all can create something we call speed? A reader's eyes, a brain that's motionless.... Speeding? – but if it all moves, at breakneck, to the universe's edge – the same speed, yes – it moves, but is forever still, it seems ... Time is speed – the war comes at its certain speed and we are lizards, waiting on our rock, and when we die we're fixed as shadows on the rock ... where we had hoped to take the sun.'

Where is this getting us? What's more important – expanding our thoughts on this, or on the world war we're here to see beginning? We're wrong, wrong about everything.

'If you were me,' says Constantin, 'You'd ask 'What happens to the workers' cause, enunciated in terms of justice – fairness, possibly – and truth? Either you accept things as they are – the pyramid, the bottom strata, the exploited, the discarded, outliers – for ever unjust, unfair, corrupted; their cause forever falsified – or....'

'Yes,' I say: 'That "or" has cost a lot of lives. The struggle. Instead – it's bosses against bosses. That's who takes on your songs and poems. Calling themselves Popular. Best keep *schtum,* to live through your silent life.'

'This world war we're waiting for,' he says, 'It won't change: it will confirm. Winners and losers, those who suffer, those who profit ... It's not a movie or a book – it means we'll all be dead. Time, stories – do they go on ...? Best get our discussion right, while we're still here.'

'Go back to movies – who is in them – who you see or who you don't?' I say. 'Unnerving, the motor, its invisible cylinders. On it drives, unstoppable. It knows its destination. And books – they're written to maintain a speed, internally; however quick you read, *your* time can't change the time they run.... Unlike movies, of course, they're still there after a day or two: no single person produces them, but you don't think of them.... You're in the book,' I say: 'But the movie? No! It's full of people and their voices – who'd hear you shout? You don't even know the plot, you're dull and ugly, don't strip off so well – and if you're shot – you die! No last words, no convalescing....'

'There's kissing in the cinema, of course,' he says: 'I think that is another kind of fish.'

'You can't change things,' I say: 'Once it's in print. Maybe if everything you wrote you titled it 'The Bible', people would think a bit, go slow ... or skip. Some guys say that everything's foretold. So what? Too quick? You missed it? Or you'll be dead before...?

'But as it is – write a slow book? They'd laugh at you.'

'Maybe that's so,' he says: 'Quick movies? There were lots. Set the projector wrong, and everything runs past, like it was at Daytona.'

'Except,' I say, 'Except none of this makes sense. Of course, you can still overdose. Have a world war. But movies, books – who remembers those? Only peddlers like us who have some tricks to sell. Quick, slow: the quick, the dead....'

'You know,' says Constantin, 'We're both wrong. Time is the celluloid, the stock. What goes on it, what they call History – not the spirit, but the mix of experience, action, theory, multi-coloured people, dying, diseased and muted – *that* is the "movie". What moves.

'History's the script: – not time. Time doesn't move. Or know.

'This is what you wish: that we were in a movie about the war that ends the world. Our world. History writes us in – the crowd. The movie ends, we are alive, Time is ready for a new scenario – it always is. We're dead, but only in the film. You'd hope for that. You're wrong.'

There is a flaw in all this reasoning, I'm sure.

*

On two nearby mountain tops there rises up on each a coil of light grey smoke, a curl of hair: the last before complete baldness.

'That's it,' says Constantin. 'We saw it. The next, perhaps the last, world war started here, we are the witnesses. We cannot comment, we're speechless.'

It comes spontaneous to us – we shake hands.

'We'll both be here at the end,' says Constantin.

What does that signify? The real end?

'We'll be the first and last to witness,' he explains: 'And so, this way, all the questions will be answered.'

'You'd need to change the questions – my questions,' I say, 'That's not so odd, so personal. Just logic.'

'That's what we humans always do,' he says, patting my cheek to show how he agrees: 'When one question hasn't found an answer, you change about: another question, maybe another answer. That's the wrong way. Start with the answer, find the question. *Ergo.*'

'I could do that,' I say, 'I did that, without all this,' and I point at the curls of smoke.

'You're strange,' says Constantin, 'But in a wrong way. Drive over you – no one even feels the bump. It's like "kill one person – off with your head. Twenty people – there's a line of ghouls eager to write the book. Two thousand – if you're elected to do it, they fit neat under the new office rug. Now – we're into twenty million, much much more – no one can do that by themselves, and so.... all guilty and all innocents..."'

'Don't say it's history, Constantin,' I say, starting to stroll up the slope: 'If we're not there to write it ... and there's no one there to read it....'

*

My! This cave is spacious, endless to explore, if you're in form and wriggle hard. There are no bones, no drawings on the walls, no ritual circles, no stalactites drawn up in threes and fours.

'Is it possible,' asks Constantin, 'That no one before us, when it's too late, found this fine void, where they could start off everything again? Or – just start off something different, just as it comes, develops. Even small, or tiny?

'Art, religion, surviving in the dark ... waiting for you and me....'

'Drawing on the walls?' I say – 'It is my *forte*. The bones –
will certainly be ours. But starting off again – oh no! Don't think
of it. Wars of succession, of religion, that English one for Jenkins'
ear – free me from all of that!'

'It could be,' says Constantin, turning solemn, prudent now –
'Our handiwork could be uncovered by people not like us at all.
Not even "people": – our hands, stencilled on the stone, not
recognised....'

'By machines,' I say: 'Sent in by people just like us – people.
Would people be hairless, or well-covered, like mammoths – in
eternal rain or snow ...?'

'There's time to work that out,' he says: 'We could run a book.
We don't have cash. If gambling's a sin, we're safe, we cannot
win or lose....'

'You can ask me, Constantin,' I say: 'I know about you,
making things up. As for me – I lived for years, unjustly accused.
If you're a suspect, you don't know if there's are grounds, a
charge ... Do you just look suspicious? A turn of phrase, grimace?
Your life proceeds, but is it steered, determined by some office
guy – the obstacles inflating, friendships dropped, the lovers
fleeting off ... promotions and rewards denied ...?'

'I understand all that,' he says: 'We've both been fired, like
automatic guns – over, over, and again. It's true, when I ended up
in journalism, I found how easily I can exaggerate to make a story.
Stories are all like that, or else they're conversation.

'But – you can't invent a fresh world war: – that's why I got
sent out here. No inventions, just the drama, truth incorporated....
But you – you could protest....'

'Who to?' I ask: 'Write letters? No one tells, you're on the list
– or maybe not: you never know. You, like everyone, are
untrustworthy, subversive. There is an answer, though. You can
submit. Avoid denouncing a whole project that you've worked for
and believed in? Don't betray – consent: that you're a useful idiot.
Agree, that you're pariah, a guilty hound. Confess.

'The cart rolls on. Maybe you lost your faith, or some of it, betrayed a doubt, maintained a principle you never told ... it's useless, you can forget all that, the nuances, the reserves....

'I did it different. I manufactured, provided evidence that made a case. I turned my innocence to guilt. No more injustice – only, the accusation had come before the crime could be committed – or even be conceived. Injustice was righted – I did everything I'd ever be accused of – not with deeds, but mental, even philosophical, commitments.

'My treachery, subversion, proved beyond doubt. It resulted from the accusation. Accused of spying when you don't? Then do it, spy – you're not a thief, but if you're jailed – then lose your innocence – pilfer all you can. It's a cure. You can resent what you have done.... feel stupid, traduced, misunderstood ... Just brush that off.'

'It's quite perverse,' says Constantin, 'But yes, I understand: it works. You beat the rap. Do what you're accused of, take the punishment. Why not? The system sails ahead, justice is done, you keep the secret since the sequence, timing, the false accusing, cannot be revealed. Except....'

'Yes,' I say, 'You do what you're accused of – maybe in the name of justice, but probably – from guilt. The sentiment of culpability ... original sin – or mischief, irreverence, perhaps. Objectively, not subjectively, you make yourself a guilty party.

'Why? From inclination: retribution and revenge. There's reasons for treason, spying – they keep the balance. So, confess, repeat offences, justify them ... do jail time, be a hero, a symbol, even a partner of both sides. Clear it all out ... and no harm done, except – to you yourself.'

*

'We've no money, and no food,' I say: 'Does that mean we're poor?'

'You can't do poor, my friend,' says Constantin, 'You jazz it up. Me, I avoid poverty: – that niggling assignment.

'There's nothing here to buy, if we were millionaires. Neither of us would kill a creature, if there were one. Eat it raw? Maybe, at the end, but not before. So, our lives will be artistic, possibly, but short.

'With water, no food, we might last a month.'

'If the war is quickly won,' I say, 'They might come, look for us – take us back – heroes or prisoners, or one of each.'

It seems unlikely. Who? And how?

We'd better do the drawings quick. Frescoes grandiose, to be photographed or chiselled off.

There must be money there, if we could identify a way.... and if there is a future.... But that's what we never could –when we were alive: find the winning angle.

I make an excuse, go back into the dark – to cry, to urinate. Water is plentiful – I'm full of it.

'Don't pollute the flow,' shouts Constantin.

'That movie guy,' I think, 'Or is Constantin thinking of the brother? Suicide. Or victim of a prank, like rich successful people often face ... Boredom, miscalculation, *accidie*.... Brilliant, self-deprecating, self-destructive? Why does he see me in the actor? In that dark place which we two have found, the cave? Did we believe in it, the civilisation? Did we represent it, seek an alternative?

'Am I a star for him – or just ambitious and morose? Mistaking me for someone else?'

I shout – 'If we're rescued, there are great roles waiting for us. But – I bet they'll choose top names instead, and puff them....

'We could win Oscars – not in our names, of course. It'd be strange – having suffered reality, to be replaced by some guys suffering quite different, closely directed stuff, on camera on the set. Here – cold and wet ... there, very hot, steered by a script, and dry.

'They might kill themselves, with the fame, the strain – except you say they're dead already.... their originals, who they really are....'

'That's the stage for you,' says Constantin, laughing: 'I'm sure they'll remember, come for us. Our names are on the payroll....'

He seems convinced.

One or both will spend eternity as prisoners of war ...

Neither of us is the escaping kind.

'It's majestic, Constantin,' I say: 'The silence. The immense tragedy, unchronicled, unparalleled.

'The end of empires, of a species – that crowed, flapped tattered wings, trod down the other species – fired tiny bullets at the universe, questioned, was sceptical, indifferent and gullible – thought it was everything and now we know – it dies like ants beneath a poison stream ... The silence: like in abattoirs, nobility reduced to little plasticated packs....'

'That's rhetoric,' he says: 'Are you so sure? The majesty? All those who hoped, who joined the military, who hid, who changed their names, their nationality ... who were not interested, not at all, in all the fallen splendour you describe? Who clung to their own selves, like we two do, like sailors holding on the masts of a wrecked, a sinking, ship ... who cower like we do in whatever cave they manage to invent ... powerless, unheard, lamented for a second, then lamenting ... You're quite right – it's silence. That's the awesome part....'

'We're professionals now,' I say: 'We could shout – send out opinions, reflections. Do our job, show courage. Make our mark, leave our names – not just palm-prints.

'Some smart guys down, far down, in a hole, they thought it up. Genetically mixed, maybe they're all heteros, looking forward to the screw that gratifies and carries on the species, they phased us out, the sceptical, the underachieving: the unclear.

'Safer by far than scrambling into space-suits, a rocket – telling some fall-guy: "light the blue paper and stand back – too bad you're not a chosen one ... All sacrifice is noble, as they say in chicken farms ... You're on your own – now make the closing speech, too bad there's no one left to cheer – except for us, the prompters ... we'll take a note. And have a laugh...."'

Pretend they're the last guys – see what rhetoric spews out: what was it for, what was it worth, what made the world worth exterminating ... Too easy, to make your enemies.

'Maybe,' says Constantin, 'We found the answer – with this protecting cave, except....'

'No food, no offspring ... no network, just two frightened brains,' I say: 'The typical mistake of primitives. It's classical – the answer to disaster's clear, but humans aren't the ones to make it happen. The lesson and the failure, packed in one. We hit the wall and "splat!" we go. The war itself – is silent, but, we must assume, definitive: the end.'

'Originality,' he says: 'We have none. All we do, is write about life – sliced very thin, and very spiced. Peppery. Everyone who's ever read us must recognise the scene – we bring the tired splintered furniture to the fore. A murder holds the stage – and yet....

'And yet,' I say, 'If you're the murdered guy, you can't take part. If you're the murderer – what a storm! Of fears, reliefs, the dread, the guilt – the being in the eye. Being the hero, villain, as you've never done before – the worm, the eagle, both at once? We can't propose. The murdered one is mute – the murderer's part, the starring role– we cannot take. The editor, the readers – the roaming eye – they won't allow. So – what? So – who? The life is all around us, fired up, burnt, destroyed, and ready to regenerate – a terrible experience, common as ash and smoke, destruction and happenstance ... We should come to terms with that – life, decomposed, recomposed, forever changed and inadmissible, not recognised and censured ... opera with real knives, the bloodied victims taking bows – without applause ... the cold cream takes off everything, the red, the black.

'We can't write about it, the centre, kernel. Ours is a tut-tut, the punishment is all. And yet – a travesty, dear Constantin! What happens in the world is dull, routine – the sentiments, the inner flow and flood ... we're not prepared to recognise it, it won't sell ... and yet – this is the crux ... our fear, the terror of living through, of being in the dream, the horror, breathing, sweating – unspeakable, and incommunicable ... despite it all – in it!'

'Of course,' says Constantin, brushing me aside: 'But of course – you've done it all. Everything that happens, and has not. We always do. Not just journalists, people who write, write down everything that happens and does not. You – and I – we filed our copy days ago. The world ends – "here's my version". Or "No! It doesn't end – here's the alternative!"

'We needn't bother – it's all art, not quite literature, but change the font, the frame, put swirls and scrolls – and it will do: what's happened ... and what's not. "Read all about – not 'it', perhaps, but 'something else'" that takes your fancy – something that's anything but life as we are living it, inside our skins....'

'The day the fire comes, and the days – it doesn't.'

Is and is not – the thinnest line. Wait! Everything will come, is all piled up, and waiting....

I say – 'What do we want to be? I'm not into becoming a white worm, that hangs in darkness, drinking dripping scum. A bat? I'm clumsy. That navigational tool – for supersonic pilots.

'I'm sure I couldn't master it. No – I see myself outside, a beetle, digging – tunnels, resting places – a crèche, a larder. A sequence of good rooms and gardens ... cellars, a *camera-obscura*....'

'Why that?' he asks: 'Cave life is ahead of us, but for you, you stroll off, avoid what is happening – life for you persists, light and dark, soil and air – the cave is one-dimensional and stark ... your nightmare....'

'The books,' I say: 'When you are very young, all happens in the forest. The nursery animals live there, the princess and the ogre, the woodcutter and the wolf. The forest is the universal place where everything can happen, magic and excess, the cuddles and the curdling of your blood.'

'It's a grand theme' says Constantin: 'Almost, you could boast – entrusted to us. To write ... embellish, make unforgettable....'

'To cave, to scratch,' I say: 'We would be known – but we're forever the unknown. Writers. No public – we write about them, the so-called public. What was done, what we were, how we rose and fell ... Behind the mask, another mask – the author....'

'The falling,' says Constantin: 'The suffering. We'll be experts. Of course, only one of us need suffer. The other – with a rock can do the therapy, the kill

'Somebody must write The End, dear friend: – it's just there's no one to sign off for the executioner.

'We are men, males, there is no hope at all of procreation, of continuity – no sequel to the epic. No, no resurrection.'

'It could be,' I say, 'That when you or I has killed the other – a rock could be rigged up – to ensure a suicide. Just sit and give a tug. The End complete ...That is the answer. There's no question. It's art, that's all.'

We sit in silence, think it over.

The last white rhinos – extinct, no war required, just dwindling out....

Extinct when things were getting good for the rare animals – the lumbering, the cute ... even the humans had their dedicated nurses, trying to cure, to straighten up, to stick back limbs, glass eyes and plastic hearts. Cry a little when it didn't work.

'Yes,' says Constantin: 'You might call it paradox – though it's not. Each individual becomes extinct, and often there's a funeral. A species, though – where does it matter, what mourns, and why? The system – everyone is needed, has a place, except quite near the end the system must go on without....

'Scarcity. When things go scarce, they get a value. When things – people – plead, ingratiate, demand – they grow a hook, a handle, an empathy. Fish people in. So, are they worth more?'

'Self love?' I say: 'Without it, no one would carve or scribble. Humans notch the stick, to show they count and calculate – moving on by dynasties and generations, instead of simple live and die. Bully and submit.

'Narcissism. When we carve, we carve ourselves:– quite naked. Not riding in our motor-cars or making phone calls – just our unclothed selves, straightened up and trim.'

Dominating all the rest. Land, sea – even air....

'But us,' Constantin insists: 'We *are* special. We're the audience for the opera. We are a special part of it, although everyone has seen the exact same thing – which still is totally different for each. We don't pretend, we just sit firm, committed not to go on stage, not to suffer, not to patronise, not to be bored. We two are umpires – between what is done on stage, and how the crowd reacts.'

'Not so,' I say: 'The show – we are the show, not what's on the stage. We all have a poacher's sack of memories – what is it worth, for anyone at all?'

'It's all we have, and it is valueless,' I say.

'We shall leave a record,' says Constantin 'But not expecting that it will be found. That is art. We haven't reached that level yet. We're ordinary, my friend. Food, drink, death. Not wanting to be animals....'

'Yes,' I say, 'It's a suburban chat. We should aim much higher. And, Constantin – do we have a mystery to leave to science?

Some genetic curiosity? In death, can we be more interesting than in our life? Can we be traces of another species, cohabiting with Neanderthal and Sapiens – like the Denisova clans?'

'No,' he cuts me short, 'We've none of that. Our bones, along with other millions, some with rings, a shroud of skin, tattooed – gathered in a sack, tossed down the precipice, off to the ossuary

'Nothing outstanding – not like the little boy they buried in the sand, holding his favourite blue stone ... They loved him, not us.'

'Listen,' says Constantin, 'Be serious. How was your piece? *I* said however it will end, you must apportion blame. That's the only way to reason, you might say it's moralistic....'

'Oh,' I say, 'I said wherever lies the blame, it's been a tragedy. No one wanted the destruction of all sides – they'd even thought of mechanisms to deter.... It seems they didn't work. Well, too late now, but as there's no one left to take responsibility.... Must it die with us, the struggle, armed, on paper and in silence? All that engaged us, inspired – all gone in the leather sack, that will hold everything – the stars, the time, the distance – everything stuffed in, before the Lord Cleaner starts to scatter out another universe.... and in the distance you can see row upon row of leather sacks, each full as an egg, each tied with a sky-blue cord....

'I realise responsibility's always abstract,' says Constantin, paying no heed: 'I insist, though – the transgressor: find where evil lies.... You, my friend, have sentiment, an empathy – so, probably, you will back off.'

*

'I see you,' says Constantin, 'As a person who likes power. You would deny it, but it fills your days – the practise, or the possibility, advantages and pleasures. A curious pleasure: an odd search – for orgasm, or castration? To you, the powerful are vulnerable, but they can take you in, destroy you. You're left anxious, dissatisfied – and never to be satisfied. Never knowing what you want – because what you want is gambling on what you want. Not knowing what will win....'

'And you moralists?' I ask, intrigued: 'With values....'

'Oh,' he says, 'That's quite banal. We're used to things that don't end well. The values – they remain, unchanged. You try upholding them, but in the end, they're bigger, more remote, than you. I don't expect to change the world, or anything at all. I'm judge – what's happened is brought before me, and I sentence. I don't have a handle on the crime, or foiling it. Judgement is outside crime and punishment: you identify the crime, punish the criminal. But your judgement – that's what counts.'

'Wanting to win, wanting to be the referee?' I ask. 'I emphasise the risk. Bring everything down around your ears – the consequences are disastrous. So, where do values enter in?

'We all will end. The values don't,' he says: 'They can't. To you, it seems irrelevant....'

'Blame, responsibility, evil – I'm interested in the consequences. Forget the blame, the values – it's all inconsequential,' I say: 'The hero rescuing the princess – but who destroys the palace, kills the white peacocks and the elephants? The evil princess who beheads her suitors – miscalculates, miscounts – and does for the last one, the lover who should share her throne? What then? Who profits? Unintended consequences ... of values or of none....'

'This doesn't attach to me,' says Constantin: 'It's details. I think we could spend our last days reflecting on life, and we'd not go a step beyond the first guys. They knew everything. They didn't know what they could do about the consequences – and so, it seems, we don't either. We're all *sapiens* – and we don't have a band-aid or a can of sardines. And nor did they.'

'We invented lots of things that you can't see,' I say: '"Destiny". "Mind". The good life, the bad life. The strategies to live them out, either one ... The sadness. How to respond?

Acceptance, resistance? Those don't help at all except – you can elaborate indefinitely on an abstraction. The point is, that you're limited to your first step, your *a priori*. The aim is limited – to win, all notwithstanding. There's no way of questioning that at all – all subsequent reasoning can be good or bad, false or shaky – but you must accept the ground, the starting place – or reject it and what follows, absolutely.'

'So,' says Constantin, 'All speculation, all speculative philosophy....'

'Yes,' I say: 'Not a waste of time, because we don't know what time is "for".'

'Survival. Anecdotes ... tall stories, lies ...' says Constantin: 'Those are your proposals for passing it – the time.'

'Yes,' I say: 'Exactly. Movies – if you have the cash and lots of guys well qualified. Poetry if not.'

'Let's be serious,' he says: 'We all die, so let's not grieve. Think of delaying....'

'These big birds,' I say, 'That fly over, falter, and fall down. We could eat them – but, they're poison. Look at what they've had to eat ... to breathe. And yet – in their crops, there must be seeds. Let's gather them, and start a plot ... a field, an orchard. Even – a farm....'

We laugh. It's not a pleasant task – but here we have the undigested seeds.

Who knows what they'd bring?

'It could be hemlock, cannabis,' says Constantin.

It's not. The black birds' seeds come up – all flowers.

'We'll try again,' I say: 'We're high up here – the air is thin. The birds, the animals you might eat – they usually run down, down where the water goes, where they all gather, and there's confabulation, misery is shared.'

I say – 'Constantin – you're straight. No doubt promiscuous while searching for a life-time partner and security – it's good,

although a paradox. Best to be sated while you seek your paradise
– that ageing flame to flicker out along with yours....'

'For your consumption, yes, I'm straight,' he says: 'When it's
required. Let's not complicate our fate with unsatisfied desires –
the flesh must wither separate, alone,' he says ... and pats my
hand, 'Or sated and forgetting....'

I press on: 'My own strategy,' I say, 'When in a crowded, even
hostile space ... is "watch the eating process". Aim for the
moderate, the cultivated: perhaps the more discriminating, less
desired. Not avid, and not hungry. I seek an adventure, even – a
trek. Not a skirmish and a rout. Someone who stacks low on her
plate – no ribs and broccoli. Artichokes are out, asparagus – is
in....'

'What a creep you are, my friend,' says Constantin, roaring
with laughter, the first time he's tried out his full laugh since we
got here. 'What tame discreet events you know! You, old roué,
who sights an isolated sail, separate her from her fleet, accost her
at the buffet....

'And do you have success, my friend?'

'No,' I say: 'It's just my fantasy. The kind of article you write
to pass the time, to pay accounts. I take what comes. There isn't
much. It's good. You don't need challenges.'

'It irks me to say, will irk you to hear, but, my friend – you're
slight,' says Constantin. 'Light and slender'.

'Me and the world – I'm in it, I can't deny,' I say.

'I can agree,' says Constantin, 'That power is given
irresponsibly, with plaudits and procedures, to people who can
calculate and plan – who make a step too far, and fall, and lose it
all, and bring us down with them, a load of offal, bones and hair
that buries them and us, and brings down too the less vainglorious
ones, the other side – who haven't risked as much. Then comes
the final throw, the bet that breaks them, all the other players,
everyone....'

'I know them, and I dread, I fear them, Constantin,' I say.

'I know them and despise them, but I have a side,' he says. 'I want my side, despite it all, to win. Humankind has a morality, along with all its other stuff – I choose a side for that....'

He kicks out at the flowers the black birds carried in their throat, the pastel petals ... The chill thin air has left the stems, the colours, pale and weak, but still they struggle on.

'Listen,' says Constantin, 'This is us two, talked through, talked out. We need some company, to change the tune.'

I agree. 'If they're imaginary, there will be space. One cave will do, unless....'

'Survivors wouldn't climb up here;' he says: 'In modernity, there's not caves enough to give one each to everyone. One cave, one clan. The rest – must hugger-mugger on.

'As for you, you have no substance. Slight. A feather, falling from a falling wing.'

We must prepare for the two strangers – maybe there'll be more. Imagination knows no numbers ... 'We should dig a hole,' I say, 'Hide our crap, what's left of the black birds, our cooking efforts, those feather crowns ... they'll think....'

'Oh,' says Constantin, 'I didn't think they'd think. And then there's who is who's: if we are patriarchs, or if we're hugger-mugger, free not to decide. The best freedom that there is, no hook, no eyes....'

'Don't ask about the war, the consequences,' I say: 'When there is trauma, you don't ask, just let the story take its walk, in its own time ... We know the catastrophe the humans come from, or we wouldn't have imagined us and them like this ... We have no alternative, no choice, '

'Helen, Sabrine,' says Constantin.

'No,' I say: 'Absolutely not. You may glimpse them, struggling upwards, towards the cave – no doubt they're worthy creatures, creations, wholly, excessively, human even – summoned up to keep us company ... to do who knows what. Cleanse your mind of them, Constantin.

'It would be a gross indulgence, to have them change our destiny. To re-create a world, their world?

'Think Niniveh, Constantin. Bigger than Budapest. Think of those vast Neolithic cities on the Russian steppe – vigorous for centuries, more industrious than Trenton or than Gary ...

'We can imagine only figments, escaping from our massacre.... scorched and reamed through ... or made pristine by our humble sadness, our loneliness ... Remember the re-build, if you dare to think of a new trial, a restoration of cooperation. Progress? Our pacific side? Can you found dynasties, lay out huge cities, disappeared, but in their long times they were huge termite hills of labour and injustice, submission to the faiths and whims of generations – surely, never to be exhumed ... those were created, buried, rediscovered, misinterpreted, forgotten and ignored ... for the best reason. Do you want these ladies to heft mud bricks, build, re-build, all this?

'Repetition – it teaches nothing....

'The vision, Constantin: where did it go?' I plough on: 'Ours, the vision? from we two who reason, hungry but still whole? Our courage, our fortitude – where did we abandon those? We are the chroniclers, remember that.

'And are those two spectres, fine creatures as they are, your inventions – is that all we can evoke? Helen, the great Beast, the first inciter of our continental wars ... Sabrine, our lovely mother who will bear and nourish us again, over and over. Make us dependent, sentimental ... Old figurines....'

He's somewhat chastened. 'We can wait,' he says.

'No,' I say: 'No myth, no saga. No dreams. We know them all. Enough.'

*

'There was a promise,' says Constantin, 'No more Floods.'

'No more regeneration, no more promises,' I say: 'The end –
believe in that. It seems that you believe there was a start, a
history, a plot – planned and not improvised. So – be tough, be
realistic.... Remember – if we'd had notice, we could have
explored the cave, survived – penetrating way back, where
nothing bad could enter. It wasn't so. We were well informed –
the best! And here we are, quite unprepared and terrified. Warning
a-plenty. Did it serve? No, not at all.'

I sense a threat, and proceed. '"Talk of the Devil", my grannie
said, 'And you'll find them there, Him and his troupe, every last
one of them, there on your back, under your skin, in your clothes,
and in your bed....'

'You named them, Constantin: Helen and Sabrine. They must
come when called. What you name and summon – even if you
think you have invented everything – they come. There's no way
to rid yourself, they'll be always with you.

'Not that I believe, of course, but there it is. Invent these potent
characters that you think will change, dictate, your destiny – and
you're stuck with them.... Witches, like they call themselves ...
they've nothing against you, nothing in particular. They live
better, that's all, and they're ok. It's you who's wavering, at risk
– it is the fear, Constantin.'

We stare into the emptiness, we're gloomier than usual.

Helen, Sabrine – maybe they are already here – deep in the
cave, we hear a flickering of laughter, smells of camphor, bleach
and salvia, it's much too dark and narrow to investigate the
tunnels, that run off the main space of the cave ...

'Suppose we go down in a city, walk around, see what's been
happening,' says Constantin, quite uncertainly, I think.

'If we need to walk,' I say, 'We won't see much. You know
how it is – these places aren't made to walk around in. They're
made to hurry through. You don't want people on the streets, it

isn't safe, they're unpredictable – there's all sorts, loitering and striding, up to no good or to everybody's good – we wouldn't know. If there was nobody, how they are doing, if they are well, or been displaced ... You might get an idea, if the buildings haven't fallen down. Or if there's a place where you can sell old things, odd shoes....'

'You know,' says Constantin, 'I think like this – those guys were so many, so attracted to be together, the more you are, the more there's wealth – and so it went, and then they found they'd made a cage – a cage to put the people who did dirty work, or none at all, and wandered round, and begged, or swept, and buried you, or oversaw your cure, your therapy – and then it was they saw they'd made a cage for everyone, themselves as well ... Or rather – a poor cage for the poor, a rich cage for the others. But you and I, my friend, we were the in-betweens. We struggled, squeezed out of the poor cage and never quite managed to get up on the high shelf, where the rich cage stood. And there was fear, a little fear but always there, that maybe we'd fall back and go where we'd been escaping from....'

'All that is done and finished.' I say: 'If by chance it gets much cooler here, and if it doesn't rain and snow so much – it means there's far less people round. So, down below, they're not making poisonous stuff like once they did....'

There's not much comment we can make. That will take years and years, we'd better start to make a notch for every day and week – except 'The week!' says Constantin, and laughs: 'It doesn't matter any more. Maybe the years, if we can make them through....'

'The neolithics, Constantin,' I say: 'They lived a bit like us – they had a patch of peas and oats ... you can survive on those, not to old age, but to a fair stretch. Enough to achieve the average – six kids, and keep the show afloat – assurance against the hot and cold, the blight, the wars – you can go on for years and years, if there's the soil....'

'They say that they had pets,' he says: 'A fox, a rabbit – maybe a wolf-dog, raised from a cub. If times are hard, maybe you eat them, but meanwhile ...

'There's dealing with the others, naturally,' I say: 'The bullies and the neighbours – maybe you get to be a bully too. Shamans and priests – that's pretty good to be. Soothsayers? I'd keep off that trade, there's resentment when you get it wrong. Music and poetry – steady but underpaid, and there's the practise and the times when you don't earn at all....'

'Nothing for us,' says Constantin. 'We'd do exactly what we did before – live teetering, and on the edge – there's always jail, or worse. We've been through that.'

'For us, a civilisation holds no hope,' I say: 'That's why we stand outside. Our profession – is to see it chase its tail, destroy itself and recreate another that can grasp that tail, and round and round....

'I spent my life, hoping there could be change, reforms that gave the power – first to the workers – that turned out vain. Then to the marginals, poor things ... that too. Then I saw – the hope that white guys, socialists, would give the secret to the rest, that all would be transformed....'

'Transformed it is,' says Constantin, 'But not at all like that....'

'And now I see – either there is war, and everything's annihilated,' I say. 'Or there is not – and all goes on until something will make it fall – implode, explode. Or nothing. Just two frightened guys, living in a cave. And dying there.

'There is another way. A new struggle, that I'm not part of, cannot be – the fight of prisoners, for liberty, the mass of people who will never scale the ladder, who will descend, be alienated, policed, watched and imprisoned ... People unknown, unknowing – off our map, out of our atlas.'

'It's happening in America,' he says, 'And what there is of Europe, and its pools of post-colonials, armed and terrified ... but the guys you think will rise – they're already in their box – in

China, India ... Or they're corralled and pacified, isolated into a reserve.

'Stand firm. All is hard, like life ... and then.... it's done. And off you go, what happens next, you'll never know.'

'Illusions of success,' I continue for him, 'Complicity in all the failures – and in what you can call encouragement.'

'A white guy in a cave,' he says, as we both laugh – 'The last rebel, even a revolutionary – no one to polemicise against.... You, the great survivor....'

'You'll do, Constantin,' I say, laughing: 'Your cold eye – sees little gain, much blame.'

'Don't complain,' says Constantin: 'Some years ago, we could have been the couple that enjoyed eternity in paradise – in Eden, anyway. A tweak on one of us, and we'd have been a pair, a woman and a man who'd leave a bone to show that everybody who came next – the total *Sapiens* – was ours, related. One big family.

'Just to decide – which of us is Eve, and off we go!'

'Don't forget,' I say, 'We started off with stars – the cinema. Now – the days of celluloid are done. We couldn't even make a pop-corn poke ... A movie of our day? Twelve hours of time that passes, seeps away.'

'When did it start,' he asks me, 'To go wrong? The big wars before this one? The despots? The invention of the state, the lines demarcating territory? The tattoos, the branding? Abductions and displacements, the treks, the flights? Invention of Spirit and the spirits – what's invisible makes good pretexts for innovation, persecution and destruction....'

'It must come from the start,' I say: 'Intelligence. Philosophy and art. The brains developing – but no answers to the larger puzzles – the purposes, the goals ... the universe ... the end.

'Possessions, property. Even the idea – of mortality ... Death is the back fence – you can't cross it, so you must make a noise, rage against it, against extinction; rage against the future, not being here, not leaving anything. Rage against the past, against the rites – your burial in a hole, clinkers in a vase.... against being a big cheese and mute and underground, with your best shield and sword. No eyes, no tongue – nothing to see, no one who listens.

'When everybody knew we were impermanent, we made the children, occupied the land, tamed the animals to carry us into someone else's territory. We pressed onwards, insured a future, because we knew *we*'d not be there, be air and dust.

'So, it ends up here. With us two.'

'There'll be another time,' says Constantin, turning away, unmoved.

'We're lucky, Constantin,' I say: 'We were here when it all went bad. That is the story, and we're in it, not comfortable, but resigned. What'd we do if someone, some guy, comes up the mountain, says he a survivor?'

'We'd know he'd not seen much,' says Constantin, 'Or he wouldn't have survived.'

'I'd be suspicious, yes,' I say: 'He's probably lied – but why? It's like when you're in Mali, and some guy says he walked across the desert, survived the Sahel, went to Europe and came back – and only ever walked. We people made the desert, Constantin,' I say, 'Or rather – someone did, so the poor people couldn't get to Europe. That someone made the people black, so they'd stand out, so they only fit with guys like them, poor, and black.

'And then there is the madness. People who say they went and then came back, and walked – they end up mad. Maybe they started so. But to be poor, black, and mad, and say you walked across the desert.... you are finished!'

'I didn't know you were in Africa,' says Constantin, with some respect. And then perhaps he sees the joke – how I might say I'd been, and walked across the desert, and I'm mad, as a result, or as a cause.

'And now,' I say, 'I'm here on this mountain. Waiting for a guy to walk up here and say "It's bad down there, up here, it should be pretty good, at any rate, I walked...."'

'Yes,' says Constantin, 'That way you'd know he lied, or maybe he was mad. At least, you won't find women who'd be stupid, real stupid enough to climb up here and think to find two guys like us, sitting in a cave and eating peas and oats ... It'd be a guy who comes, for sure. Scared, neurotic. That kind – we do not want.'

'It's humiliating, Constantin,' I say: 'Surviving. Pegging out – not *in* the action, but deceased because of it ... Armed struggle? Not a chance!'

'Any catastrophe would be humiliating,' he says: 'One day waking, going to work – then you and everybody else – a heap of ash. No time to ask, "What? Who?" Like termites when a flame-thrower burns down their nest.'

'Don't bury me, Constantin,' I say. It sounds nonsensical. 'I mean – not you, and not in a shallow pit you dug. You'd look absurd, scrabbling. I'd want to be not buried, but hidden away; as if I might one day be visited. Put me somewhere, out of sight, but do it quick, and leave me suspended there....'

'You're not suspended: you're not there,' he says: 'There's no room now for 'do this': you'd have nothing to communicate. Accept what comes – or don't. It's all the same.'

'Each of us,' I say, 'Could contrive a story. It would be something indestructible that we could leave behind, that showed we were here, invented a story and so – were not here, not at all. Not for ever. We'd have left.'

'Oh,' says Constantin, 'Mine will be about a train. When it ends, I'll climb aboard, and off I'll go. No ticket – who cares? I'll go to jail for that....'

'Mine will be to show I don't exist,' I say.

'Pouf,' he says, 'All stories are about that.'

'Too bad,' I say, 'That way – I shan't die here, and maybe shan't die anywhere at all. The proof of my existence is the tale that I invent – and everybody sees it's not a proof of anything at all.... It's a proof that I'm a story, I'm not me. Judgement – is suspended. Here, not here. Who can tell?'

'Except,' he says, 'There's no one else. Silence.

'It's not at all the movie – I saw it one afternoon – 'After the end of the world' – and there was a crew, and music, actors – the whole shoot. It proved the world had not ended, not at all! There was a cautionary enterprise! An awful movie, though....'

'My story, Constantin,' I say, 'Will have no characters at all. Just names. That shows it's not about us, nor anybody, no one at all. It fails, and so I'd need to invent another tale – which also isn't about us. And so, and so – becoming a Sheherazade, and she has never existed, not in this world – world ended or going strong. Perhaps....'

'You know, my friend,' he says: 'Your life has been a long catastrophe. The people you depend on hate you for your being smart – too smart for them, you break all holds, you are not arrogant, not ambitious – just a well-oiled wrestler who is never pinned.... And so – they make you suffer. In every way, they defraud you, ignore you, humiliate: – "too slick to live". All you care about is the eye that watches that you never cheat.

'The perpetual exam? A con, another fraud – you are the only candidate. The test – to show that you exist ... Or that you don't, and so you are immortal.

'You never lose, there's no one to beat you ... No one for you to beat. The prize? A hand-grenade, the pin removed – it's yours to hold and carry off the stage ... the proof you live; or once you lived....'

'Oh no,' I say, 'The prize is the examiner – the lovely prof, the object of desire of any, every, kind ... The eye. The judgement eye. You need that, and everything – is yours!

'You're in your tale, you write it down, obsessed, and he and she walks up and down, inspires – and ah! lays out the scent of musk, the fields of flowers that start with just one word – you must define, refine, sharpen that word to start the tale, lay out the landscape, and on and on you go – that word grounds a system, an encyclopedia, a dictionary of every word that's ever spoken, a phenomenology of thought; a picture of everything at every age and after; when it's disappeared or rusted out – a construct bigger by far than any living universe, an invention that grows and grows, and hatches stars and galaxies that flit and fleet like mayflies and have my paper people living on them for seconds when they can create – '

'What?' he asks: 'You see? Created what? Everyone you needed, who had power over you, they hated you. They saw they didn't matter, not at all, they couldn't boss you. You didn't put them, not one, in any story that you conjured up. Their powers were silly – and they stamped on you....

I conclude, '... they can create ladders to the farther stars ... Those stars are small and cold – no bigger than a gold armchair....'

'Nothing,' says Constantin: 'You take us nowhere.'

'You can't ride me, Constantin,' I say: 'I am not a horse. I free horses.'

That's it. We must accept. We can't get out, not even by telling tales.

*

'Back where we started our examination, of who we were, were like,' he says: 'Our ancestors found hallucigens. That's how they invented civilisation. They were forever spaced right out. Maybe we could lick these rocks, take off....'

'I'm not sure about that,' I say, 'I don't want, don't need that kind of trip ... And you – you don't really want the colour wheel, you want the fog. It covers what you know – the truth.'

But he insists. 'Grow.' Mushrooms? Berries?

Nothing.

Much remains. The earth is inaccessible, so if it empties, no harm done. The other mysteries, the galaxies – they carry on. We two – our little brains are standard size, hundreds of other people, quite like us, fit in. Hypothesise: – there's places we have never seen in life, but they too – we can imagine them, their residents – all's grist. We "know" – and never see them. Constantin is legalistic, so he needs a structure for his thoughts – on structures he can hang his tales, a bundle of the history that gives, shares out, the blame. His brain projects these structures anywhere there's room ... and so....

'You're more intelligent than me,' I say.

'I know,' he says: 'It doesn't change things, not by much. I see where you don't, which of your schemes will fail. That's all.'

'We're getting weaker, Constantin,' I say, not wanting to follow him into my precinct.

'It's a blessing if we are,' he says: 'We don't want to linger. And it's better if it's natural, just flickering out.'

'We could have a conversation,' I say: 'Like – which is faster, horse or camel?'

'Mule or donkey?' he replies.

'And more intelligent?' I ask.

'Ah, intelligence,' he says: 'They all are beasts of burden – their intelligence is limited to who rolls smoother with their natural powers, who is more natural. The horse – you have to train its shoulders. They're the weakest point, and if you do it wrong, you spoil the animal for good. Camels resist. If they tire, they let you know – and by that time, you're nearly dead yourself....'

'A mule can't have a family,' I say: 'That's pretty smart.'

'Or lucky,' Constantin agrees.

'I got taken to the track,' I say: 'I loved to see the animals, but not to bet....'

'That's idiotic,' says Constantin: 'You in a nutshell. People, bright people, bet to show they understand: – the mathematics, and the qualities, the powers, of every animal. It isn't chance, unless you're reckless. It's finding several orders, putting them together – the weather and the going, the owners, trainers: – the contenders, their four legs. Then the judging of the animals – how they are built, trained and ridden – how do they look ... and so and so. Not to bet shows you are not a proper human, not exercising the human powers of estimating, judging, risking, following your reason....'

'I'm humbled, Constantin,' I say: 'I thought it was just ignorance ... not liking to lose money, even.'

He turns furious, and makes to hit me....

'You don't understand,' he shouts: 'It took us millions of years – we worked to make the mental tools precise, reliable, and you, you throw them all away! Ah, the horses – they are beautiful, you think, and there it ends.... Impressions, leaps in the dark....'

'The war,' I say: 'The ugliness, the cruelty....'

'Will it come, and why?' he asks, rhetorically: 'The interests, resources ... courage and superficiality.... The sides – they grow alike – and menacing. Nationalisms against each other; fear of the strangers, vainglory – a little *facho*, a lot cowardly ... what is the vision? Where do you find it? Past or future? History – must depend on who writes it, reads it? How does it weigh the various substances?

'The people you call leaders – what do they despise, mistrust the most: – the people led, or their own colleagues? Their aim? To gain, or not to lose? To win and make a peace, to lose and plan revenge? What do they plan to play – a game of chess, or darts, or football? Do you attack, scheme out the weakness, play your best game on your own, or have the referee, the historian, on your side ... changing the rules, the ball's bounces left to fortune....

'You see, my stupid friend –'

'Of course I see,' I say: 'It ended as we know. We weren't engaged, no analyses or prejudice: we were not asked. Our brain – it made no difference at all.... Was it intelligence or folly did for us, and all the rest – poor animals? Most likely, both. Smart, locked in: undeviating.'

He hits me quite hard with his fist. My mouth – it bleeds, the teeth already loose, fall out.

'There!' he says: 'Do an analysis on that. Who is to blame? Your provocation and stupidity, or my principles, the laws...?'

'I don't accept your premises,' I say. It comes out as a mumble. I pick a rock, to hit him back, but he picks up a larger one, big enough to crush a skull. Too bad, we're weak – we circle, facing off, our arms are tired, we sit and squat, we pant, the image swims.

At night, it's dank. We sleep cuddled in each others' arms. By day, we speak little, hide away, and sometimes fight like mountain goats – without the horns.

We could ban the use of those big stones. Or just exclude first use, except – if someone uses them first and someone else replies, that is the end, as we found out. It's best to use first massively, and go to live deep underground. To break your word is not so grave, if those not first off dead, survive.

'What blame, and what responsibility,' I ask, 'If you break your word, eliminate the other side, what then? Is survival a big wild card, that beats the rest, and justifies....'

'Oh,' he says, 'Forget all that. I never dealt with what is justified. Always – there's vengeance, the past a poacher's sack of insults, claims, slights and defeats – all unavenged, or insufficiently – and there are threats, that can be used to justify....'

'It's right,' I add: 'The past gives reason space to play today, tomorrow....'

'To what end?' he asks: 'Causes, effects and consequences – I'd never say a moral vantage justifies all action and reaction.

Being in moral credit – in theory, gives you no ticket to break the moral law. The law, that is, that you – and maybe me – identify.

'Responsibility and justice – they don't hang together. I am a judge, but have no power, no law, no court. Justice for me – identifies, that's all, it has no means of punishing, of exacting what? Ancestors' reputations re-evaluated...?'

'So,' I say: 'The answer is, if there's a winning side – be on it. If there are surviving sides – be on one of them. How do you fix it? In our case – what's to be done?'

'We have to see,' says Constantin.

'Surviving,' I say, 'Is repetition, the gateway to eternal return. We are in the land of Nietzsche, of the devil's "loneliest loneliness".'

'Going through the gateway – is not something we can do,' he says, 'Not by ourselves – it must be written, scripted, in to what is, will be. What happens.

'The gateway – doesn't open up on to a garden, new. The garden's been already laid out, we were expelled for ever, and now there's the garden once again, just like there always is ...

'Life as the cave,' I say, 'Life as peas and oats. If we want to evaluate Nietzsche – we couldn't be positioned better.'

'Well,' says Constantin, 'I don't want that. I'm not so clever or so well read.'

'It's certainly likely, though,' I say, 'That, if history repeated, and we came to the war once more, its beginning and its end – our end – it would repeat. The cycle, circle, would repeat –infinitely.

'It's like a prayer wheel – you twirl the wheel, the prayer is written on a scrap inside – and off it goes, round, round as many times as you have patience for. It's us, the humankind – that's how we are. It may even be a species thing, and not a universal one – if we were jaguars, maybe the spectacle would go on and on, all different, longer, uniform – but as we are, it will go round and round. We're in the wheel, we're written down, we can't be changed.... A prayer. In a wheel.'

'You are confused,' says Constantin, 'There is no gateway. No explosion. It's an hypothesis, and *that* is justified because it is. When it happens, then, it's not hypothesis.'

'It is a consequence,' I say: 'The chain must have an end, which is its start – and here we are, we two. No one will come up to see if we're alive. We'll die, and down there on the plain they'll build the big steppe city, eat peas and oats, something will happen, something terrible, and those who're left will drag the carts over the mountains and do battle with the people there, herders, mobilise light cavalry, try out their bows and arrows, and so ... Everywhere.... If you don't believe me – you can dig it up.'

'You're terribly literal,' says Constantin, and laughs. 'It's like you must have a somewhere, a spot on a map, as if in some way you were authenticated by cartography. Relax! You're not nowhere, you're somewhere, and so, unique and irreplaceable ...

'And yet – it isn't so, you realise. You're irreplaceable but you don't recognise yourself – none of us does, while all our lookalikes stand on the stage and say our lines. We sit inside our skin, look out, settled in our seat, we die our deaths, like millions of Madame Butterflies, like Monarchs, millions, forever returning identical, to those tall identical trees.... all different and the same....'

'OK,' I say: 'Roughly said, but – we know all that. We've seen the script, the good folio – and there's no need for us here, or anywhere, except we're like the Monarchs, we have infinite identical existences, stories, because logic and sentiment are identical, unchanging, and you and I, as individuals – we are identical....'

'Of course,' he says: 'The individual starts as a rough-cast, undeveloped. The developing individual must grow like all others, the developed individuals. That's why you and I – we are identical. You, my dear, and I – are one. We feel, we reason – in exactly the same way. It has to be. It is.'

'So,' I say, 'The development must be identical, and so – it must repeat, the exact, identical, same way. Time is a loop. The monkeys knew. There they were, and now – here we are, and here they are, and then we've gone, and they go too....'

We sit and contemplate. No one comes up the mountain-side, no one developing, developed. No one at all.

'Russians?' I ask. More like us than we are, we're more like them every day. What are they like? What are we like? We're good at making enemies – if we tried not?

'Chinese? Do we have what they want, whatever that will be?

'Where did it all start, Constantin? What did we want, where did we want to go, "we", all of us, like toads, climbing over each others' backs. It escapes me, but clearly everybody knew where it would end and no one, nobody at all, seems to have wanted it, except....'

'I can't answer you,' he says: 'Someone made an error, overplayed a hand ... exaggerated. Those who played it straight, only reacted, no aggression ... did it play out well? Was that good strategy?

'Ask a chess master – better to defend, or to attack? That's not the point – the point's the win. Winning must be good, or there would be no point. There's lots of Masters, and they'll all have lost. Some lose to robots, maybe we, everybody, did; or did we win?'

'There's less blame if you lose, you said. What game is that?' I ask.

'That's all I can conclude,' he says: 'It's not the whole story. You might have miscalculated. The aim? To enslave everyone you can. But then – the slaves are in your house, they write your letters and your books, they are your soldiers and your counsellors. The slaves have slaves. They do the work, design the smart machines.

'Even if you kill those marked as slaves – you'll meet resistance on a larger scale, and in the end, you always lose. Is the destruction worth it?

'Worth? There is no prize: – to win – the only aim. The rest is loot and plunder, and revenge.'

'I feel I should be comforted,' I say: 'Except....'

'Exactly so,' says Constantin: 'The sentiments, the fear, the apprehension – those gnaw you, erode you, as they must, or else, there'd be no point. The drama must be cataclysmic, it's your death being played out on the stage ...

On every mountain top, at sea, in glass bubbles under lakes – in twos and threes, the last humans discuss the end, the good and bad things the species had achieved ... the world is full of them, survivors, gurus and philosophers of every kind.... Millions. 'Why were we spared? How can we leave our mark? Our deaths – will they be noticed, if so, how and where ...? Who will come next and try the joust – immortality the prize, and yet – as it was said, 'if it's not forever, there is no point' – and yet: and yet, it never is forever. Not for anyone, nor anything.

We're always the last humans. No need for a war. Sad animals who discuss accomplishments. What if....

'We've eaten poison for weeks,' says Constantin: 'What if we go down to the plain. We're immune, or dying. Take the consequence. If it's all ended and there's only us – we can make a conclusion, a plus and minus. If we're wrong, and it's all gone on, we've been forgotten. We're two Van Winkles – sheepish, owed back pay. Needing a haircut.

'Back into the background, like before, no fuss, and no conclusions.'

'I wouldn't dream of starting off,' I say, 'If there's no purpose, and it's not for ever. If the end is written in, if there's no plan – I don't see a point. It's like watching lizards, geckos – climbing the wall, flicking a tongue, pause ... climbing, running.... disappearing.'

'It sounds like you are giving up,' he says.

There's some satisfaction in his insight – he has lasted better, longer. Hope is the nourishment. He's squirreled away a box of it, 'hope', for personal use.

'Those eyes in the sky,' says Constantin, 'That we can't see. Who's watching them? Or us? Suppose we make a show. They'd maybe send a person, down from the stars, perhaps....'

It seems unlikely. 'A show?' I ask, 'A rave? A shout – we could dig out a mouth, down to the fire to make a tongue, and use the ash for teeth. Help! Do we need it? Of course, but not without conditions and hohums.

'Or stage a drama – those last. People remember what's fantastic, although they've no imagination ... that's why they go to theatres. We'd be a prince with ghosts....'

'We are the ghosts,' says Constantin: 'Too many. It's better say "a star is born". I told you – if you could stay off dope, you'd have an ordinary life, perhaps. Your death-wish means I should survive, if there is any justice.

'They might spy on us – and see you bursting out – arias, soliloquies. A presence always pulls a crowd ... You're the big bag of wind.

'If anyone is left alive – guys hear the rustle of the cash, the fusion option everyone has hoped will come: a name the ordinary crew can puff. The universal hope is for miracles – divinities ... Those keep the secrets in a pouch. They're niggardly. They could deploy a special food for when we've cooked the animals, and plants are dry ... Energy? Perhaps appliances you don't plug in, but warm and boil in sympathy with us, as we just walk around, and talk philosophy....'

'For sure,' I say, encouraging him: 'The gods step in when there's a crisis. We'd keep free will, but, with a bunch of guys immortal and omnipotent, jiving and parleying on the street – the sceptical choice is out. To be agnostic, you'd need be blind. The proofs of godhead – they'd come knocking on your door, distributing free pills and smokes....'

We laugh. But how ... how to attract attention that we want, and not the crowds of fans, and whitecoats taking samples from our heads ...?

'My friend,' says Constantin, wheedling, dropping his suspicions and hostility – 'We need our sanity. It isn't help, salvation, that we want. Nor suicide. We need an answer. Why? Who made it end like this, and was there ever an alternative?

'In the books, the everlasting scrolls – it always ends in fire, in meltdown. Then, in darkness, exhaustion of the land, resources – yet ... here we are. For us – it's been the darkness first: – the overhang, the cave – the mountains tall as skyscrapers, the sun that cannot penetrate. The others – they will have seen the fire, entered it and disappeared.'

I'm terrified.

'I cannot tell, I'm quite unsure,' I say: 'The "if", the "why". We two know our destiny, but – what's the context? I don't know, and nor do you.'

'My fear ...' I begin and stop ... is being alone with Constantin, the raging credulous terrorising Constantin. My fear is being alone with him – without him, without anyone.

'Each of us,' he says, 'Inside, has a wasps' nest of individuals. They are at various stages – you might say they're jujubes, allsorts, a pick'n mix of people who will talk to you and mostly say what is coherent, more or less compatible – with what you want and what you've heard ... What you fear is – you. You. Being alone with them, who's you.

'You are not, not ever, you alone – you're a picture, piece of scenery ... a surface with a painted garden or a lake, even a battlefield, and then behind – some struts and stretchers and a base that lets you move around and stand up straight. Straight, in every context. You're like all those who use, use dope – you do it because you know you're straight, dull as a river mist.

'Getaway? Some hope!'

We are quite weak. Both – more than a little crazy. I suspect – instead of flickering out, each has the same idea – when the other dies, and there is no one left – the last survivor will climb down ... Go down to the plain, see what the war has left. Maybe – they're all alive – and suffering, of course, going extinct, like everything, but humming, strumming, making cash and betting it, shooting and shouting. Life! The world!

We're not good subjects, neither one – too intense, too sceptical. But – both cling on ... my twin, my Constantin – he'll die and I shall take him on and carry him with me, until The End.

Leave his bones in the cave, my drawings on the walls, go down. See how they're doing.

About the author

John Fraser lives near Rome. Previously, he worked in England and Canada.